Tyrant
OF THE
Badlands

SIGMUND BROUWER

BETHANYHOUSE
MINNEAPOLIS, MINNESOTA

Tyrant of the Badlands
Copyright © 2002
Sigmund Brouwer

Cover illustration by Chris Ellison
Cover design by Lookout Design Group, Inc.

Published by Bethany House Publishers
11400 Hampshire Avenue South
Bloomington, Minnesota 55438
www.bethanyhouse.com

Bethany House Publishers is a Division of
Baker Book House Company, Grand Rapids, Michigan.

Printed in the United States of America

Library of Congress Cataloging-in-Publication Data

Brouwer, Sigmund, 1959-
    Tyrant of the badlands / by Sigmund Brouwer.
        p.   cm. — (Accidental detectives)
    Summary: Twelve-year-old Ricky goes undercover in Alberta, Canada, to infiltrate the gang of thugs that are thought to be vandalizing his great-aunt's mobile home park.
    ISBN 0-7642-2567-7
    [1. Mystery and detective stories.   2. Alberta—Fiction.
3. Vandalism—Fiction.   4. Kidnapping—Fiction.   5. Gangs—Fiction.
6. Christian life—Fiction.] I. Title.   II. Series: Brouwer, Sigmund, 1959- .
Accidental detectives.
    PZ7.B79984Ty   2002
    [Fic]—dc21   2002010719

SIGMUND BROUWER is the award-winning author of scores of books. He speaks to kids around the continent in an effort to instill good reading and writing habits in the next generation. Sigmund and his wife, Cindy Morgan, divide their time between Tennessee and Alberta, Canada.

For Olivia
and the sunshine you bring
into this world

CHAPTER  1

Mike Andrews and I sat on the couch, watching Saturday morning television. Mike kept flicking his eyes at a huge fly banging against the window. Without warning, he grabbed the remote control from my hand and snapped off the television.

"Um, hello?" I said.

"Look," he said, "Grown-ups tell us it's a waste of time to watch television all day, right?"

If Mike Andrews—redheaded and with the middle name of Trouble—opens with a question when he already knows the answer, he has a scheme cooking.

Normally I don't mind Mike's schemes. Except for the painfully bright mixture of colors he always seems to wear and the bad jokes he comes up with, you can hardly ask for more in a best friend.

Only now I wasn't interested in trouble. We were in the family room of my house, and there was no way I could leave for any trouble to happen somewhere else. Somewhere safer.

"Couldn't this wait until Joel's not around?" I asked. My little sister, Rachel, was with some neighbors, and I was baby-sitting because Mom and Dad were taking a mini-break, something they did one Saturday a month. They spent the entire day together, like best friends, just enjoying each other's company. Yuck—romance between parents.

Mike left the couch and paced back and forth. "Genius has no patience, pal," he said. "Besides, Joel's got his video games downstairs. We won't disturb him."

"Obviously," I said, "you've decided to forget everything you know about my little brother."

Joel's six. I'm twelve. Even with that six-year disadvantage, Joel scares me. He's almost invisible. He spies on me all the time and shows up and disappears again when I least expect it or want it, giving me atomic heart attacks. He has this old teddy bear he carries everywhere. Threatening to take it away from him is my only defense.

"All right," Mike said, "even if Joel shows up, what harm can he do?"

I rolled my eyes and shook my head with a loud sigh at Mike's silly question.

"Well," he said, "it's not like I'm planning anything that will go wrong."

"Sure. Should I remind you about that watermelon and the giant slingshot?"

Mike winced. "Slight miscalculation."

Slight, all right. We'd buried a wheelbarrow so only the handles showed, then cut a car tire tube open. We'd attached one end of that giant rubber band to one handle, the other end of the tire tube to the other wheelbarrow handle, and had ourselves the world's largest slingshot. Which would have been fine, except the watermelon we fired went a little farther than we expected.

"So tell me, Mike," I said, not caring that he could hear distrust in my voice, "what's on your mind now?"

"Ten thousand dollars."

"Right," I said. "And after that, instead of getting on an airplane for next week's trip to Canada, we'll flap our arms and fly like birds to visit my grandfather."

"Funny you should say that word," he said, grinning his usual pumpkin-sized grin.

"What word?"

"Fly." Mike pointed at the window where the big black fly still bumped against the glass. "That's how we're going to win our money."

"Start from the beginning," I told him. "You've lost me somewhere."

"*America's Funniest Home Videos*," he said. "You know, the television show. We'll send them the best video of the year."

"Sure," I said, not meaning it.

"I've already decided I'm going to buy a motorcycle for when I'm old enough to drive it. Yeah, our parents are going to tell us to save our winnings, but with all that money, I bet I can talk them into letting me spend a little of it on fun stuff."

"Um, Mike?"

"Yes, Ricky?"

"One slight detail." I stood up, walked over, held his chin with one hand, and slapped his face gently with my other hand. "This is your wake-up call. You can't spend money you haven't won. Don't you think there are a billion people all trying to send in a funny home video?"

"Shhhhh!" He walked away from me toward the fly at the window. He watched for several seconds, then, with one quick swipe of his hand, he scooped the fly into his fist. He walked back to me and held his fist close to my ear. I heard the muted buzzing of the fly.

"Look, pal," he said. "All we need are about twenty more flies. You got a jar we can keep them in?"

"Then what?"

"Not much. After we've got the flies, we need Popsicle sticks and glue."

"Then what?"

"We'll need your parents' camcorder to videotape."

"Then what?" I've learned not to trust Mike when he doesn't tell me everything up front.

He explained. I whistled in admiration.

"You're right," I said. "What could go wrong?"

CHAPTER 2

It took us a half hour to catch the flies we needed. During that time I peeked once in a while to see if Joel was still playing video games on the computer. He was, hardly noticing me opening and closing the door each time.

After catching the flies, we worked on the Popsicle sticks while the flies cooled down in the freezer. Finally, another fifteen minutes later, we were ready.

Mike and I looked down on the low coffee table near the television and surveyed the results of our work. There was a small, simple airplane made of two Popsicle sticks glued together in the shape of a cross. Along the top of the wing of that airplane we had placed twenty dabs of glue, evenly spaced and now almost dry. Beside the airplane was a pair of long tweezers and the jar of nearly frozen flies we'd just taken from the freezer.

"Go easy on the little guys," Mike warned as I opened the lid. "You don't want to hurt them."

"Like sticking them in the freezer was good for them?"

He ignored my sarcasm. "If these don't wake up, we won't freeze the next ones as much."

I wasn't sure I had the patience to catch another bunch of flies, so I hoped we'd guessed right on how long it would take to knock the flies out without killing them.

I opened the jar. I lowered the tweezers into the jar and, as gently as possible, lifted a fly by the wings.

Mike brought the airplane closer, and I lowered the fly—skinny legs down—onto the first dab of glue. Without pausing to admire my handiwork, I went for the second fly. Then the third. Fourth. . . .

Five minutes later I was finished.

Mike set the airplane back on the table. I grabbed the nearby camcorder and zoomed in on the airplane. There in my viewfinder, neatly lined up across the top of the Popsicle-stick wing, were the twenty flies, each stuck into a dab of glue.

"As soon as the first one twitches," Mike said, "roll the film. The rest will be waking up soon."

"You got it, pal," I said. My enthusiasm was growing. I couldn't think of anything that might go wrong with this. We'd have the most incredible video ever. Maybe it would actually win a contest. And money. For once, Mike had actually come up with a good idea.

All we had to do was wait and watch.

Finally the first fly twitched into wakefulness. It buzzed its wings as it struggled to free itself from the glue. The same with the second fly. The third. Within seconds, all the flies were buzzing and trying to fly.

I had the camcorder rolling.

Twenty flies. All trying to pull themselves from the glue. Would it work?

Yes! The sound track on the camcorder probably caught the whispers of awe that left our mouths as the Popsicle airplane actually began to lift into the air.

"Too cool!" Mike blurted. "I can't believe it!"

I didn't answer. I was too busy trying to focus the camcorder as I kept the rising airplane in the viewfinder.

The background became a blur for me as I attempted to keep the airplane as large as possible in the viewfinder. The plane rose higher, well above my shoulders. I had to crane my head backward to get every detail.

The flies began to lose their energy, and the airplane slowly drifted downward again. It headed toward me.

What a great shot! A fly-powered Popsicle airplane flying right into the camera. *Step back slowly, step back slowly*—

"Aaaaaack!" My foot landed on something that pulled out from under me. I began to fall. All I knew as I was falling was that I had to protect the camcorder. I pulled it into me to wrap it in my arms and braced for the pain.

Because I couldn't throw my arms out to break my fall, I crashed too heavily into the side of a chair. The chair in turn toppled into the bookshelf. The bookshelf tilted. I could only watch in horror as it tumbled down, scattering books like autumn leaves.

Mike dived for the shelf, but it was too late. The top of the bookshelf smashed into a ledge near the television. Books flew out. Heavy, hardcover books.

About a half dozen of the books tumbled into the small aquarium on the ledge. And the aquarium, of course, smashed down on the floor.

So much for Mike's great idea.

CHAPTER 3

I couldn't speak. Broken glass sparkled like diamonds. Water drained in all directions. Fish flopped against the carpet.

"Sorry," Joel said, breaking the silence. "But you stepped on my hand."

"Hand?!" I squeaked. "You're supposed to be playing video games. Not crawling around the corner of the family room to spy on me."

"The screen's too small," Joel said. "My eyes got tired. The fly plane is a good idea, though. Maybe someday I'll do this and make a present for Mom."

He gravely watched our goldfish flopping on the water-soaked carpet among the books and scattered pieces of broken glass. "Or maybe not. My eyes feel good again. Time to get back."

He scooted back out of sight.

Six-year-olds have no sense of responsibility.

I caught a movement out of the corner of my eye. It was Mike, edging toward the hallway to make his escape, too.

"Freeze right there," I ordered. "You're helping me

out of this mess."

He gave me a sick smile. "Of course."

I set the camcorder down in a safe place and nodded. "I was supposed to baby-sit all day. Which means we have until five to clean this up. Get the fish into a bowl of water. They should live until you buy another aquarium."

"Me? Buy another aquarium?"

"I'll give you my leftover allowance money. While you're going to the store to get the exact same size aquarium as this one, I'll be cleaning up."

He grinned.

"And I know exactly how far away the pet store is," I warned. "So don't think you can show up three hours from now."

His grin dimmed. Silly of him to think I didn't know his tricks.

Mike was back sooner than I expected. All in all, the disaster could have been worse. I got the bookshelf straightened—no nicks. I put all the books in place—hardly any water on the covers.

With large towels, I blotted the carpet as dry as I could, and I vacuumed the glass pieces too small to pick up by hand. After that I set up a fan to blow the carpet dry. I threw the towels in the dryer and then folded them when they were done.

The goldfish survived and made it into the new aquarium. None of the aquarium knickknacks had been damaged by the fall. There was no way for anyone to tell it was a new aquarium.

We finished an hour before Mom and Dad showed up.

"Not a bad day's work, pal," Mike said as he headed out the

door. "We can be a couple of busy beavers when we need to be."

I shook hands in agreement with him. For once, I had survived his trouble.

Until eight o'clock that night.

"Hey, Stephanie," Dad called to Mom from the family room. "Will you get the kids ready? We've got to get them together to say hello to Grandfather John for his birthday."

Strange, I thought. *There's no telephone in the family room.*

My heart sank as I rounded the corner into the room. Mom was holding Rachel. Dad was holding the video camera.

"Ricky and Joel will be there next week," Dad said. "They can deliver a video of all of us singing 'Happy Birthday' to him."

The camcorder! In my earlier panic, I'd forgotten all about it.

He frowned as he tried a button on the camcorder. He raised his voice to speak to Mom. "Steph, the battery's dead."

My heart sank farther. *Dead battery? I can't have—*

"Was someone running this all afternoon?" he asked.

—let it run the whole time we were cleaning up.

Dad took the videotape out of the camcorder.

"And this tape has run to the end," Dad said. His brow crinkled. "What's on it?"

"I don't know," Mom said. "Slap it in the VCR and we'll find out."

He did.

The first thing I saw on the television was flies twitching on a Popsicle stick.

"Mom," I tried weakly, "isn't there a good movie on?"

"Not now, son." Her total attention was on the rising and falling fly-powered Popsicle-stick airplane as it cruised around the family room, with Mike and I whispering how cool it was.

The airplane disappeared in a blur as the camcorder view shot upward from the way I had fallen over Joel's hand.

His words came out clearly a few moments later. *"Sorry. But you stepped on my hand."*

Then I heard my words being played back. *"Hand?! You're supposed to be playing video games. Not crawling around the corner of the family room to spy on me."*

The room swirled again, showing when I had moved the camcorder and set it down in a safe place. Right where it could record the rest of the clean-up efforts I had frantically begun.

"Interesting," Dad said as the tape wound down. His eyebrows made a V as he glanced in my direction. "I didn't hear anyone tell us about this at the dinner table."

"Would you believe we wanted to get something ready for *America's Funniest Home Videos?*" I asked.

That's when Mom and Dad started laughing. I knew later they'd want to talk about why I had tried to clean up the mess without telling them. And I knew later I'd tell them it had not been a good thing to do. But for now they were laughing too hard to really get angry.

When Mom finally caught her breath she said to Dad, "Well, instead of videotaping the message, why don't we call my father right now? He's a couple of time zones behind. This shouldn't be too late for him."

All of us moved to the kitchen. Dad made a long-distance call to the province of Alberta in Canada, and Grandfather John answered a few rings later.

They talked.

Dad looked at me and frowned.

"Are you sure?" he said on the phone.

He listened.

"All right," Dad said. "Here, I'll put Stephanie on the phone. You explain it to her. If she says yes, it's fine with me."

Now I was frowning. This didn't sound good. Were they canceling the summer vacation we had been planning all winter?

"Stephanie," Dad said, handing her the phone, "why don't you talk to your father?"

"What is it?" she asked, covering the receiver with her hand. There was worry in her voice. The kind of worry that I felt, too.

"Well," Dad told her, "he wants Ricky to fly in a day or two earlier than the rest of his friends."

"Why?" Mom asked.

"Let him explain," Dad said. "He wants Ricky to help out your aunt Louise."

Dad looked at me. "Trust me, son. This could be good for you."

I get nervous when parents say things like that. Real nervous.

CHAPTER 4

The airplane seat beside me was empty. The pilot announced that the airplane was cruising at 32,000 feet at a ground speed of 550 miles per hour. The flight attendant stopped by for the tenth time and asked me if everything was fine. I told her for the tenth time that it was.

She smiled the kind of smile that made it seem like she wanted to reach down and pat my head. "You should be proud of yourself for traveling all this way alone."

It was Monday. I was on my second flight of the day. The first had taken me into Salt Lake City. From there, this connecting flight took me north toward the city of Calgary in Alberta, Canada.

I smiled back at the flight attendant and didn't tell her what I thought about her treating me like a baby. Mom and Dad had brought me to the check-in counter at the airport. Because it was airline policy—though I'd insisted that twelve years old meant I was fine by myself—they signed a note for the airline that explained that my grandfather would be waiting for me when the plane landed, and the airline had made sure attendants escorted me from gate to gate. Which made me grumpy. Now my only job was to sit by the window and look down on the Rocky Mountains, so it didn't feel like I had much to be proud of. Except for being polite to flight attendants who wanted to pat my head.

The flight attendant picked up my lunch tray, moved on, and left me to the view of the beautiful blues and whites of the mountain peaks below.

My thoughts went back to my grandfather, John Grant, who was waiting for me in Calgary. He was Mom's dad. Mom had been born in Canada. After high school in Alberta she'd gone to college in the United States, and there she'd met Dad, changing her last name, of course, from Grant to Kidd. Along with a new last name, she got a new home, Jamesville, and had moved away from Canada.

Mom's mother—my grandmother—had died when I was six years old. I didn't remember much about Grandmother Grant except a sweet smile and the way she had packed mud on a bumblebee sting the only summer I had visited them. Since then my grandfather had visited Jamesville a few times, but he had never stayed long, mainly because in the summer he couldn't leave his farm for very long.

In other words, I hardly knew him. I hoped it would work out to spend time alone with my grandfather. I hadn't spent much time around him, and during our short time together, he didn't say much. Dad said he was quiet because he missed my grandmother so much. The other part was something sadder. Since my grandmother had died, Dad explained, Grandfather John had turned away from anything to do with God and church. He'd become almost a stranger to the entire family.

I wondered if it would work out because I would be spending time with one stranger first—my grandfather—and then another stranger, my mom's aunt, whom I was supposed to be helping once I got to Alberta. The few days until my friends were to arrive already seemed like forever.

With homesickness settling in my stomach, I watched the Rocky Mountains as the plane flew all the way north across Montana and into the province of Alberta. The plane circled Calgary—with the mountains along the western horizon as far as I could see—and touched down with hardly a bump.

The flight attendant actually did pat my head as I left the plane, and she told me to have a good day. I told her I would do my best.

My best wasn't good enough, because things got puzzling in a hurry.

When I got to the baggage claim I saw Grandfather John striding toward me. He thanked the airline person who had brought me there, then showed his driver's license to prove he was the adult I was supposed to meet.

When we were alone, I didn't even get a chance to say hello to him.

"Take this into the nearest washroom," he said. He pushed a big paper bag into my arms. "Change into these clothes."

"Sir?"

He wasn't the kind of grandfather who gives hugs. He was tall, with thick, thick hair that was so white it almost looked like the cotton fluff on the fake beard of a department store Santa Claus. Some old people have saggy throats and double chins. He didn't. He seemed more like a cowboy from one of those old black-and-white movies.

"You're old enough to call me John," he said with a hint of a smile.

Already I felt better around him. I straightened my shoulders.

"Although you've got your luggage," he continued, "we're not quite ready to go."

"Sir?"

"I meant it when I said to call me John. You've grown plenty since I last saw you."

He pulled a pair of scissors from his back pocket.

"Sir?" I coughed. "I mean, John?"

"There's a couple fellows back in Drumheller," he said. That was the town close to his farm. "I can't take the chance they'll see you before we get you looking just right."

"John?" It was getting easier to say—unlike the flight attendant, he wasn't patting my head.

"Looking just right," he repeated. "I bought some hair dye. It should help."

"Hair dye?"

"Don't worry. The instructions say it washes out."

"Hair dye?"

He pushed me toward the men's rest room and followed behind.

Five minutes later I stepped out. My hair was cut short and ragged. It was also black instead of my usual blond. I wore black jeans, black T-shirt, and a black jean jacket. There was a plain gold earring clipped onto my left ear. I was chewing gum with my mouth open, just like my grandfather had instructed.

"Good," he said as we walked toward the exit. "Now you

look exactly the way you should."

"I do?"

He gave me his first big grin. "Yup. You're big for twelve. You look like a rotten teenager just out of jail."

CHAPTER 5

At the doors that led out to the parking area, John put his hands on my shoulders and stopped me.

"Walk different," he told me. "Bounce on your toes with each step. Swagger. Like you've got a bad attitude. And wipe the smile off your face. Sneer. Pretend like you hate the world. Remember, you're supposed to be a teenager with a jail record."

"But—" Nobody had told me anything about this part.

"I'll explain when we're in the truck."

I stepped aside to push the door open for a woman carrying a baby.

John yanked me back. He shook his fist in my face. He looked angry. My grandfather was a big man, and for a second I was scared.

His voice, though, came out much less angry than his look. "Right from the beginning—which is now— you and I have some acting to do. The sooner we pretend someone is always watching us, the better."

He kept shaking his fist. "See, I'm pretending like you just said something to make me mad. But I pulled you back to keep you from helping the woman and her baby. If the two guys I'm thinking of happened to be watching, they should believe you don't respect anything or anybody. Rotten jerks don't care about other people."

He shook his fist right under my nose. "Swing at me," he said.

"Pardon me?"

"Say 'what,' not 'pardon me.' And swing at me."

I did, trying to punch him in the stomach.

With speed that surprised me, he caught my fist in his right hand and twisted my wrist back. I didn't have to pretend it hurt. My grandfather was a strong man.

"Good," he said. "When you get outside, spit on the pavement. When we get to my truck, kick the back tire before you get inside. From here on out, you need to think you're a rotten punk. Everything you do has to reflect that."

I had so little idea of what was happening that I did everything he told me.

Between the curb and getting into my grandfather's brown Ford pickup truck—after kicking the back tire hard enough to hurt my toes—I managed to spit twice.

"This looks like it will be an interesting vacation," I said. "Although I have no idea—"

My grandfather John looked straight ahead as he spoke. "Cross your arms like you're angry and stare out the window, like you're not speaking to me. Get into the part. You're going to be living and breathing it for a few days. Start now."

He turned the key, started the truck, and shifted it into gear.

"Excellent," he said. "You really do look angry."

"I'm getting close," I said. And meant it.

Grandfather John began to laugh. "Your mother used to get that exact tone of voice when she was a teenager."

An airport bus roared past us as we drove out from the shade of the terminal into the blue of the prairie sky.

"We've got over an hour's worth of drive ahead of us," John said. "Listen to my story. By the time we get to the town of Drumheller, you decide if you want to help."

CHAPTER 6

"By the way," he said, "welcome to Alberta." He swung the truck left at a traffic light. Just like that, we were out of the city. There was a service station and a few large parking lots for airport passengers, but other than that, in three directions I saw nothing but nearly flat land and scattered trees among fields of wheat. In the fourth direction, the jagged blue edges of the Rocky Mountains made a backdrop for the Calgary skyscrapers.

"It's big," I said without thinking.

"Big?"

"The sky. It stretches and stretches. Kind of makes a person feel small."

Grandfather John chuckled. "Once you get used to it, anything else makes you feel closed in."

"I like it," I said. "The hawks must feel like free spirits high up there in the sky."

He didn't say anything for over a minute. I began to turn my head to see if I'd said anything wrong.

"You keep looking out the window, Richard, like you hate me. As we get closer to Drumheller, I don't want to take any chances." His voice was sad. "Don't mind me, either. It's just that Molly often said the sky made her feel as free as a hawk. Once in a while, I'll hear her voice when I least expect it. . . ."

Molly was my grandmother, the one I could barely remember.

"I'm sorry," I said.

"Me too," he said. "Not for what you said, but because she isn't around to see how you've grown."

I stared out the window at the land rolling by. I didn't know what to say.

A few minutes later we turned off the narrow two-lane road onto a four-lane highway.

"Which way are we headed?" John asked without warning.

"North," I said.

"Is that a guess?"

"The mountains are to our left," I said. "They were to my left as we flew north from Salt Lake City."

"And what highway is this?"

I closed my eyes and pictured the marker back at the exit onto the highway.

"Number two," I said. The truck tires began to whine higher as we gained speed.

"Keep looking away from me out the window. What am I wearing?"

Again I closed my eyes.

"Blue jeans. Dirty cowboy boots. White T-shirt with a small stain on the chest."

"I'm impressed. Your mom's right," John said. "More than

once she's told me how you notice details. Any particular reason?"

I had no idea why we were talking about these things, and I felt squirmy to be talking about myself, but I answered. "It's hard to explain. It's like I want to know as much as I can, but I don't even know why I want to know."

"Believe it or not," he said, "I understand what you're trying to say."

He paused. "Your dad tells me you want to be a writer. Maybe watching things around you is part of it."

My turn to pause.

"Well," I said, "I don't talk about it much."

"I can live with that answer. And I didn't mean to pry. I've got a reason for asking you all these questions."

"The same reason I'm dressed in black, my hair looks so bad, and I have to chew gum with my mouth wide open?"

"Same reason. Let me start from the beginning."

Ahead, at the side of the highway, I saw a speed limit sign that read 110. I remembered Canada uses kilometers per hour instead of miles per hour, and I relaxed.

"Molly's sister is still alive," John said. "That would be your great-aunt, Louise Myers. Her husband passed on a few years back and left her a small trailer park with a little convenience store. The park is a ways out of the town of Drumheller, down near the river. She runs it and makes enough to survive. There used to be fifty or so mobile homes all renting space from her. It gave her a good income, and with that many families, it kept things busy at the store. Now it's down to twenty-five homes. Some are nice. Most are run down. It's the folks with the nicer homes that have been moving. She's been forced to charge less rent just to keep the people she's got, and that means the people who've moved in lately tend to be the ones with the older mobile homes. As the neighborhood gets worse, she has to keep dropping the rent."

"Why did people start leaving in the first place?"

"The nicest homes were getting vandalized. And too many weird things have been happening."

"Weird?"

"Electricity cuts on and off for no reason. Loud noises in the middle of the night. Ground shakes. She's called the county officials to find out what's happening, but of course, whenever they are around, things look normal."

I couldn't see his face because I was staring out at passing countryside. East, the way I faced, the land rolled on in big squares of green and yellow crops. I was willing to bet I could see for fifteen or twenty miles to the horizon.

"If that wasn't bad enough, she has to deal with two stooges named Miles and Joe. They moved into the park about a year ago, and since then, they've been a real pain. They threaten people, but never enough to give her a reason to call in the police. She thinks they're the ones who vandalize the homes, but she can't prove it. They come into her store. One keeps her busy, the other steals things, but again, she can't prove it."

"Can't she kick them out?"

"She's asked them a few times, but they prepaid for two years. They've told her they'll sue unless she comes up with a good legal reason for forcing them to leave. Not only that, they told her they would break her arms with a sledgehammer."

I was surprised and nearly turned my head to look at him.

"A threat like that is against the law!"

"She can't prove they threatened her. It would be the word of the two of them against hers."

John let out a deep breath, one I heard above the tire noise and wind noise. "I just found all of this out. Louise doesn't like dragging people into her problems, but it finally got so bad she called me. At first I wanted to have a little chat with them. Louise told me it wouldn't work. As soon as I left, she said, they would bully people again. So I started to think I'd have to do this from another direction. You."

"Me?"

"Sure," he said. "Although I don't get to spend much time around your family, it doesn't mean I don't care. From conversations with your parents, I know plenty about you and your brother and baby sister. I got to thinking that it might be handy to have someone like you spend time in the trailer park. You watch for things and remember."

"I'd be a spy," I said.

"Think of it more as an undercover agent. You already know your disguise."

"A rotten teenager."

"Really rotten. Louise's already complained to neighbors that you're arriving for a week. Rumor has it that you've been bounced out of five reform schools already."

"This is a dumb question," I began, my face almost pressed against the glass, "but is it okay to be lying?"

"What do you mean?"

"I'll be pretending I'm someone I'm not. If people ask me things about my past, I'll have to lie."

He chuckled. It was a nice, warm sound. "That's a tough question. What do you think?"

"Maybe people will understand once they find out the truth when this is all over."

He chuckled again. "It's been a while since I bothered myself with troublesome questions. Let me stew on it. In the meantime . . ."

"I'll do it," I said. "I just might have fun, too."

"Understand you're only to watch and report. I don't want you doing anything to put you in danger."

"Yes," I said.

"I mean that," he said. "Miles and Joe are nobody to be messing with."

"I'll really watch out," I said.

"There's a cell phone in the glove compartment. The best and smallest I could buy. Keep it with you at all times. I'd suggest taping it to your calf."

"The calf of my leg?"

"Sure." He chuckled. "In the Wild West, cowboys used to hide weapons there. No one would ever think to roll up your pants to look for a cell phone. If you have an emergency, all you need to do is hit the power switch and call me."

I took the phone out. Grandfather John gave me his number, and I memorized it. He made me repeat it back to him five times, even though the number was already programmed into the cell.

"Good," he said. "Now, when I drop you off, the first thing you need to do is throw a rock through Louise's front window."

CHAPTER 7

"You can't make me do anything!" I shouted at Louise Myers from her front lawn. She stood across the lawn on the front porch of her mobile home. It was a new double-wide home. Pots of flowers hung from the railing around the porch. Her lawn was well trimmed, nice curtains decorated the inside of her windows, and everything around her home was neat and clean. In the sunshine of the afternoon, it looked attractive, especially compared to some of the older, sagging mobile homes in the rest of the trailer park.

"Come inside and don't make a scene," she said calmly.

"Don't tell me what to do!"

"Now, Richard . . ."

"And don't call me by that dorky name!" I shouted. "I already told you it's Rocky."

"Please," she said. "The neighbors can hear every word."

That was the whole point, of course. Our plan was to let everyone in the trailer park know I was a first-class jerk and troublemaker. She and John had already decided it would be the best way for me to establish my under-cover role. If everyone figured I was a bad kid and a loner, I had the perfect excuse to wander around at all hours. If Miles and Joe did catch me spying around, they wouldn't be worried about me reporting them because they'd think I was the kind of kid who hated authority.

Good plan or not, it felt strange yelling at Louise. She was Grandfather John's age. Her hair was brown, streaked with gray, and cut short. She wore jeans and a sweatshirt, and in the short time we'd had a chance to speak, she'd been very relaxed and friendly. I liked her. And now I was yelling at her?

"Don't push me!" I screamed. "It wasn't my idea to come here to some small town in the middle of nowhere!"

I saw an old woman two doors down step onto her lawn. She put her hands on her hips and stared at me.

"What are you looking at, lady?" I shouted in her direction. She *tsk-tsk*ed and retreated back into her home.

"Richard. You do not treat the neighbors like that. Get inside right now before I get angry."

"Oh yeah?"

I raced to the road that ran amidst all the mobile homes. I picked up a stone the size of a baseball.

"Oh yeah?" I repeated at the top of my voice. "This is what I think of you!"

I took a deep breath. I told myself that both Grandfather John and Louise wanted me to do this. Then I fired the stone as hard as I could at her big picture window.

CRASH!

"Take that!" I shouted.

I walked down the road, away from the shattered glass.

"Richard!" she called. "Richard!"

As earlier instructed, I ignored her. I still had work ahead of me.

CHAPTER 8

I walked past ten more mobile homes. Some were in the shade of tall poplar trees. Some had skirting around the bottom of the homes. A few had bales of straw piled beneath them; Louise had explained it was to keep the cold out during the winter. Some of the homes didn't have anything around the bottom, and I could see underneath where the axles had been jacked up and supported on blocks of wood.

Way ahead, past the poplar trees that lined the river at the edge of the trailer park, I saw the white and gray clay canyon walls of the valley. The mobile home park was set on the banks of the Red Deer River, a little downstream from the town of Drumheller.

I hadn't known what to expect when I was riding here in Grandfather John's truck. A half hour north of Calgary, we'd left the main highway and turned down a wide, two-lane road. Most of the rest of the way had been more fields and rolling hills. Then, without warning, the road had dropped into a narrow canyon that wound down into a deep valley that was invisible right until the drop-off.

Not only was the valley itself a surprise, but also how it looked. On top of the plateau it was gentle farmland. In the valley it was almost like a desert, with white and gray and brown eroded hills, like we'd driven onto a set for a western movie. This was the famous Badlands of Drumheller, the site of important fossil finds, home of the world-famous Royal Tyrrell Museum—the dinosaur museum.

Drumheller itself—a couple of miles up the road—had about six thousand people. Grandfather John had explained that coal mining had been big in the area, and as the coal supply vanished, people had found oil. And long, long before that, dinosaurs had roamed the entire valley.

Altogether, it would have been a great place to explore as a tourist with my friends. But instead of spending this part of my vacation with Mike and Ralphy and Lisa and Joel, I was here alone and in the process of making sure nobody would become a new friend.

I walked slowly, kicking at the dirt with my black boots.

A small boy playing in a sandbox waved at me. I almost smiled and waved back, but I remembered who I was supposed to be. I spit in his direction instead, and he stared at me with a hurt expression across his little face.

A few minutes later I reached Louise's convenience store, which was set in the middle of the trailer park. It was nothing more than a converted mobile home, lined with shelves that held the usual small items of any convenience store. A noisy freezer lined the back wall.

"Hello," a girl said as I walked past the cash register.

"Whatever," I said, not even looking in her direction. I marched down the aisle toward the freezer. I dug around for some Popsicles, scattering ice-cream bars everywhere. At the cooler I grabbed a couple of colas. At the counter I threw some chocolate bars and chips down beside the colas and Popsicles.

"I haven't seen you before," the girl said as she began to ring the items into the cash register.

I lifted my head and looked into her eyes. That was a mistake. They were hazel eyes and regarded me without blinking from a beautiful face. She was dark-haired, a couple of years older than me, and I fell instantly into a river of puppy love.

"Well—" I stopped myself. I was about to tell her how I thought it was a very nice place to visit. Then I remembered I had a job to do.

"You're quite the babe," I said. "What are you doing in a dump like this?"

Red spots of anger appeared on her cheeks. She put the items in a paper bag. "Are you always this rude?"

"Are you always goody-two-shoes?" I said. It pained me to put a sneer into my voice. It pained me to think of my ragged haircut, my black hair, and the earring clipped to my left ear.

"The total is six dollars and twenty-five cents."

I grabbed the bag. "Yeah? Charge it to Louise Myers. I don't think she's going to be feeding me tonight, so the least she can do is buy me this."

"I can't do that."

I walked around the counter.

"What are you doing?" she said, more anger in her voice.

"Where's the phone?" I saw it beneath the counter. I grabbed it and handed it to her. "Call the old lady yourself."

She dialed a number. "Louise? It's Crystal. There's a . . . a . . . *person* here who says to charge things on your account."

Crystal looked at me as she listened to Louise, her eyes like rays of fire. "Yup," Crystal answered. "Black hair. Bad attitude."

Crystal listened a few moments and hung up.

"I think you're a jerk," she said, "taking advantage of a sweet woman like Mrs. Myers."

"I think you're a jerk," I repeated, mocking her by raising my voice. I began to walk out. "Have fun working your dead-end job."

I stepped out into the bright sunshine, feeling horrible. At the rate I was going, someone was going to shoot me by the end of the day.

I wandered to the edge of the mobile home park, walked down a path to the river in back, found a huge flat rock beside the river, and stared at the flowing water. The river was about a hundred yards across and lazy brown. On the other side, narrow steep canyons were filled with shadow. Grandfather John had explained that all the canyons were formed by the runoff of water as smaller streams ran down the river and cut through the clay and sand. That's how people had been able to discover fossil sites, because the eroding land peeled down hundreds of feet to where dinosaurs had been buried for hundreds and hundreds and hundreds of centuries.

I'd been there for about half an hour, enough time to finish two colas, three chocolate bars and one-and-a-half Popsicles. I was skipping small stones into the river when two men drove up in a green truck.

"Hey, kid," a guy in a baseball cap said as he stepped out. "We hear you're a real punk."

I swallowed at the sudden dryness in my mouth.

"Yeah," the driver, a bearded guy, said. "People everywhere

are flapping about how you busted the old lady's window."

I told myself who I was supposed to be. I shrugged, looked away, and didn't answer.

The guy with the cap stepped around in front of where I was sitting. I had no choice but to look up. He was wearing a blue jean jacket with the arms cut off so it fit him like a vest. His biceps were as big as pickle jars, only pickle jars were never covered with tattoos. He reached down, grabbed my shirt, and twisted it. He straightened and lifted me to my feet.

"Didn't no one teach you to respect your elders, kid?"

"Didn't no one teach you to use deodorant?" I figured if I was going to get pounded, I might as well make it worth my while.

He gritted his teeth and brought his fist back to punch me.

The bearded guy grabbed his arm and stopped him.

"Relax, Joe," the bearded guy said. "You gotta like a kid like this."

Joe slowly set me down. I kept my face straight, pretending I wasn't as terrified as I was.

"My name is Miles," the bearded guy said. "My friend here is Joe. What's your name?"

"Rocky."

Joe snorted. "What kind of a name is Rocky?"

"One that should be easy for an idiot like you to remember." It seemed that around Joe if I showed the slightest bit of fear, I was dead. "Rocky. It only has two syllables. If you do forget, think of the stuff that you have for brains. Rock. Then you should remember."

Joe snarled. Miles laughed, reached into his shirt pocket, and pulled out a pack of cigarettes. He tapped one loose and handed it to me. "What do ya say, kid? Light up with some buddies?"

CHAPTER 9

The cigarette, of course, was like an invitation to join their little club. Grandfather John had told me not to do anything that might be dangerous, and joining them didn't seem safe. On the other hand, if these two were part of what was behind the weird things happening at the trailer court, it would be good to make friends. But on the first hand, what else would I have to do next? And then there was the fact that I'd promised Mom and Dad I would never smoke. Would it be all right to break that promise in the name of trying to help Louise? I was running out of imaginary hands to juggle my questions, getting dizzy thinking about it, and had no desire to get dizzier by putting tar and nicotine into my lungs.

And they were both staring at me, waiting for me to become their buddy.

I took the cigarette.

They smiled. The bearded guy flicked a lighter, lit his own cigarette, then Joe's. They each took a drag and squinted through the cigarette smoke. The bearded guy flicked the lighter again and brought the flame toward me.

I snapped the cigarette in two and tossed it at his feet.

"Hey!" Joe said.

"Cigarettes are for losers," I said. "Got any idea what they do to your lungs?"

Dad had told me that if you held your ground, people respected you. They might not like you or your opinion, but they'd respect your strength. I was hoping Dad was right. I wanted to be part of this little group, but I had to do it on my terms. I also had to pretend to be the tough guy, afraid of no one.

Joe reached out to grab my shirt again, but the bearded guy slapped Joe's arm downward.

"The kid's right, Joe. I've been trying to quit for years." The bearded guy grinned.

"Is it true you knocked out the woman's front window?" Miles asked.

I studied him. They were both a couple of inches taller than me. Joe was muscular and heavy. Miles was fat and heavy, but it looked like solid fat, and I decided he would be the worst one of the two if it ever came to a fight. Miles's beard was untrimmed. It covered his face almost up to his eyes. His hair was curly tight, the same darkness as his beard. When he grinned, it showed a single-tooth gap in the front of his mouth.

"I didn't knock out the window," I said. "It got in the way of a stone I was throwing."

Miles laughed. "You always this quick to look for trouble?"

"I don't like people trying to push me around."

Joe grunted. "You wasted a good throw, kid."

"Yeah? It went exactly where I wanted."

"What he means," Miles said, "is you did it for nothing. See, we'd be happy to pay you for stuff like that."

It was taking all my concentration to try to speak like Rocky. It felt like I had to pause each time to wonder what Rocky would say in this situation. The only way I'd managed it so far was to pretend I was writing a story. If Rocky was a character that I was making up, how would he react? Would he be happy at getting paid by these two?

I decided not. He would be suspicious.

"Yeah?" I said. "What's the catch?"

"No catch," Miles said. "We got this scam going around here. We could use your help."

"We got this scam *going around here."* So there *was* a reason behind everything! I wanted to ask, but I didn't want to make them suspicious.

"How much money we talking?"

Miles reached into his pocket and pulled out some bills. He peeled off some green ones, some purple ones, and some blue ones. He slapped the bills into my hand.

"Three hundred," he said. "Twenties, tens, and fives."

"Monopoly money," I said.

"Huh?"

"All these colors. Canadian money. It looks like Monopoly money." I stuffed the bills into my pocket and grinned. "But it probably spends as good as American money."

I grinned again. "All right. What do you want me to do?"

"Start a fire," Miles said. "Number 27. The owners are on vacation. It's a brown mobile home at the north end of the park. Old enough it should go up like a dead Christmas tree. We supply the gasoline. You light the match."

CHAPTER 10

Shortly after midnight I stepped out from the shadows of the front porch of Louise Myers' trailer home. The night sky dazzled me. The trailer park was poorly lit, and because of that, thousands of stars were clear and sharp against the velvet black above.

I jogged across the lawn, onto the road, and jammed my hands into my pockets. The best approach was the bold approach. No slinking from tree to tree. If anyone asked what I was doing, I'd tell him or her to mind his or her own business. Ahead, once I reached the can of gasoline Miles had told me to expect hidden beneath the porch of trailer number 27, I'd be much more cautious.

A train whistle blew in the distance. A few minutes later I heard the high-pitched yipping of coyotes in the canyons on the other side of the river. Both sounds were haunting and reminded me I was very much alone.

Very much.

All through the rest of the afternoon and early evening—after leaving Joe and Miles—I'd wandered around the trailer court, hands in my pockets, kicking gravel on the road. People would look at me, then look away. Or they'd look down their noses and frown. I couldn't be sure if they did it because they'd heard about me breaking Louise's window or simply because of the way I was dressed.

For the first time I realized what it must be like to come from a background where a person didn't have the advantages of braces for crooked teeth, new clothes, and the love of two parents together. There were plenty of kids my age who struggled in lives without baseball leagues, birthday parties, and someone in a minivan to drive you wherever you needed to go. I'd seen those kids during visits to the city and looked down my own nose at their spiked hair and earrings and ragged clothes.

This is what it felt like to be on the outside.

My worst time that day had been when a little old woman tending her flowers on her knees had called out to me. She had told me it was hot and had offered lemonade. I waved her away like I didn't care and kept stomping gravel because that's what someone like Rocky would do, but her small kindness, when everyone else was prepared to hate me, had been so powerful I'd gotten a lump in my throat.

This is what it felt like to be unloved and on the outside.

Over dinner with Louise, the only place I didn't have to keep acting like a punk with an earring, I'd described my afternoon. Louise had smiled sadly and told me she hoped I'd remember, because there would be times when I could give kindness and not know how much it meant to someone else.

As the echo of the train whistle faded I tried to put the haunting loneliness out of my head. It was tricky business, getting ready to burn down someone's home, and I didn't want to make a mistake.

I made it to number 27 without disturbing anyone. No lights came on in the homes I passed; no shouts came at me from the darkness.

Finding the can of gasoline was no problem, either. Miles and Joe had left it beside the lawnmower, so it looked completely normal to have it there.

I grabbed the handle of the can and stepped to the side of the home. I stood beneath the low-hanging branches of a tree, even though it was so dark I doubted anyone could see me from the road.

I waited.

I waited some more.

Buzzing of mosquitoes started to drive me crazy. Their bites drove me crazier. I set the gasoline down and began squashing them as soon as they landed on my face and neck and ears. It would have felt better to slap them, but I needed to be quiet.

I waited more.

Without warning, the ground vibrated. I told myself I was imagining things. But the ground actually vibrated. The branches in front of me shook slightly. Lights turned on in different homes. People inside must have felt it, too. I wondered if I also heard a low steady hum, but I couldn't be sure, not with mosquitoes dive-bombing my ears. Then, with as little warning as it had given to start, the vibrating of the ground quit.

I was trying to figure it out when I saw the dark outline of a man walking down the road. There was another smaller outline in front of him. A German shepherd guard dog. On a leash held by the man. It was the new security guard that Grandfather John had suggested Louise hire.

Perfect.

I waited until he and the dog were near, then moved away from the tree and toward the house. I lit a match.

"You!" the man shouted.

I dropped the gasoline can and stepped back from the house.

"You!" he shouted again.

At his shouting, lights went on in the mobile home next to this one.

"Hey, you!"

I turned and started to run.

"Freeze!" he screamed. "Or I let the dog loose!"

I froze.

CHAPTER 11

The security guard shone his flashlight right into my eyes. "Good thing Mrs. Myers hired me this afternoon," he said. "One night on the job and already I've earned my pay!"

"If you give me your report card," I said, remembering I was supposed to be a tough punk, "I'll put some silver stars on it for you."

"You got a smart mouth. But you won't be so mouthy when all the trouble hits. I caught you red-handed with a gasoline can. You were going to burn that house!"

"You can't prove it," I said. Because he was shining the light in my face, I couldn't see much of him. By his voice, he sounded young. It also sounded like he had asthma. Unless it was the guard dog panting. "I'll tell the judge I needed the gasoline for something else. I was just borrowing it from where the can was left beside the lawnmower."

"Likely story," he said. "Come with me."

"Where?"

"To Mrs. Myers. She owns the trailer park. She

hired me. She can decide what to do with you."

"Good," I said. "I'm staying with her."

"Huh?"

Before I could explain, the porch light next door snapped on. There was a creaking of screen door hinges. A woman in slippers and a frilly pink housecoat marched out. Her hair was in curlers. As she got closer, I saw she had a skinny, pinched face.

"Who are you?" she demanded of the security guard.

"Night-Thru Security," he said.

"We don't have security here."

"Out of Calgary," he said. "Just hired today. And I caught this boy with matches and a gasoline can."

She turned her voice toward me. "You're that punk I heard about. I hope they lock you up and throw away the key."

If I really were a kid named Rocky, I'd have told her I'd be glad to spend time in jail if it meant getting away from her. But I couldn't force myself to get quite that nasty, so I kept my mouth shut.

"Mark my words," she said, "you're going to end up roasting in the fire with the devil."

"Ma'am," the security guard said, "sorry for disturbing your sleep. I'll take him away now."

"You didn't disturb me none. I was reading my Bible. And don't interrupt my Christian duty. I'm witnessing to this evil boy."

Witnessing?

She shook a bony finger at me. "Boy, if you don't want to roast forever, you listen to me good."

The security guard took my elbow and tried pulling me away.

She grabbed my other arm and held me. The guard dog growled.

"Boy, turn away from the devil." She glared at the guard dog until it quieted. She glared at me. "Believe in Jesus and you shall be saved."

"Ma'am, really, we should be going and—"

"Shut your mouth," she snapped at the security guard. "I'm witnessing, and this boy needs to hear about the love of Jesus."

I didn't feel much love coming from her. I wondered how someone who didn't know about God's true love could ever believe, hearing it from her.

"Believe in Jesus and you shall be saved," she repeated, like it was a bumper sticker message.

I tried to imagine what someone like Rocky might think of her witnessing. I said, "I'll be saved from a poor home and jail sentences and getting beat up by gangs? Just by saying I believe, it will erase all the bad things that have happened to me and all the bad things ahead?"

I was getting angry at her bumper sticker religion, just like Rocky would have gotten mad. "Tell me, lady, how does believing in Jesus make my life better?"

"The devil made you ask that question! Believe in Jesus, boy. Run! Run from the devil!"

"Good idea, ma'am," the security guard said. "We're on our way."

He yanked me from her grip and, in a fast walk, we left her behind.

When we got far enough away, the security guard spoke to

me in a friendly, quiet voice. "I go to church myself, but she'd be enough to keep me away if I didn't already believe. I'd be happy to try to explain a little better if you're interested."

We stepped into the pool of light beneath one of the street lights. I was able to see him clearly. He had a chubby, shiny face, and his uniform stretched across a big belly.

"Whatever you want to get someone to believe," I told him, remembering something my dad always told me, "witnessing with words is one of the weakest ways."

The security guard stopped and squinted at me in surprise. "Pardon me?"

I realized I'd stopped chewing my gum with my mouth open and that I'd forgotten to speak in a nasty voice. I had to convince him not to like me.

"I said, 'all fat guys are deaf.'" I spit on the ground. "Why'd you ask? Can't *you* hear?"

His face tightened with anger, and he pushed me ahead of him.

An hour later, after the security guard had left me with Louise, after she and I had discussed my capture over late-night hot chocolate, I was lying in bed, staring at the ceiling, and asking myself the same question I'd asked the shrill lady in the pink housecoat.

How did believing in Jesus make life better?

It was a question I fell asleep with. I didn't wake to an answer but instead to hard tapping on my window.

It was Miles and Joe. At four-fifteen in the morning. And they wanted me outside.

CHAPTER 12

As I slipped into my black pants and T-shirt, I planned what I would say to them. I opened my bedroom door and started to walk down the hallway.

"Ricky?" Louise whispered from her own bedroom. I was surprised she was such a light sleeper.

"It's Joe and Miles," I explained. "Outside. They want to talk to me."

"They're earlier than we expected," she said. "Be careful."

"I will." In the afternoon, when I had told Louise about the money I was getting paid to burn the trailer, she and Grandfather John had come up with the solution—hiring a security guard on short notice. Because the security guard had caught me, to Miles and Joe it looked like I had really meant to do the job, but the trailer was still safe. Our guess was that Miles and Joe would ask me about it as soon as possible.

Which, of course, was now.

I was almost at the door when I remembered. My earring!

I rushed back to my bedroom and clipped it into

place. *If they'd seen me without it . . .*

A few minutes later I found them beneath a large tree in the back of the yard. I told myself my heart was pounding just because I'd hurried to get there. Not because I was so afraid my throat felt like it was being squeezed by rubber bands.

"You sure took your time," Joe said in a mean voice, his face lost in the shadow of his baseball cap.

"I should punch your lights out," I said, trying to act as tough as Rocky would, giving them the answer I had prepared. "You jerks didn't warn me about a security guard."

Joe brought his fist back. "You little—"

"Easy," Miles told Joe. "The kid has got a right to be mad."

To me, Miles said, "Kid, we were just as surprised as you were. She's never had security around here before."

"Find out first if the brat squealed on us," Joe said. "Then we'll see who's got a right to be mad. Then he'll really get a surprise."

I heard a click, about waist high. Joe moved his hand out of the shadows. It didn't take a genius to figure the "click" had come from his switchblade, which now gleamed dangerously in the moonlight.

"Unfortunately for you, kid," Miles said, "Joe has a point." Miles smiled without humor. "No pun intended. We've got to know what you told the security guard and old lady Myers. We saw him catch you. We saw him pull you into the old lady's trailer. What we don't know is what you told them about us."

"You were spying on me!" Rocky, I told myself, would get angry at this.

"Of course we were," Miles said. "We got bigger and better

things in mind for you. Torching the old trailer was a test. Now, tell us, did you squeal?"

"Of course not," I said. "I don't help no one."

"We'll find out by tomorrow if you're lying," Miles said. "If you did squeal, you might as well tell us now."

"I didn't squeal. Do you see any cops around? Old lady Myers is trying to keep this quiet. Just like I did."

"Even if you did squeal," Joe said, "it's your word against ours. You can't prove we paid you to do it. Two against one, you'd lose."

"Get this through your little pea-brain," I told Joe. "I didn't squeal. And here's another thing you might as well figure out. I'm keeping the three hundred dollars. It's your fault I didn't know about the security guard."

I didn't enjoy being Rocky around nice people, but it sure was fun pushing Joe.

"Miles, let me pound him," Joe pleaded. "Just once."

"Put the switchblade away, Joe. We can use this kid."

"Yeah?" I said. "How much money you got?"

"As much as it takes, kid. Trust me, as much as it takes."

"So what do you want next?" It had only been this morning that Grandfather John had warned me to watch without getting involved. But things were going so good and it seemed I was getting so close, I wanted to hear what they had in mind.

"Did you happen to feel the ground shake just before the security guard nabbed you?"

I nodded yes to Miles's question, trying to keep a straight face to hide my excitement. What was I going to learn about the mysterious shaking?

"Well," he said, "night after next there's some major

digging planned. Major enough that the ground is really going to do some hopping. What we're going to need from you is a big diversion so that no one notices."

"What kind of diversion?" I asked.

"What kind of diversion?" he repeated. "Let's put it this way. About a thousand dollars' worth."

CHAPTER  13

"Digging?" Louise Myers repeated. "What kind of digging?"

It was Tuesday morning, and I was sitting at the breakfast table. She sat across from me, a coffee cup halfway to her mouth and a thoughtful expression on her face. I swallowed a mouthful of scrambled eggs.

"I don't know," I answered. "From what Miles said, it sounded like digging made the ground shake. So I guess it would have to mean heavy digging, with big equipment."

She shook her head no. Her hair was pulled back with a kerchief. "I can't recall seeing any bulldozers or things like that."

"When do you first remember it happening?" I asked. "The ground shaking at night?"

"About a year ago."

"When Joe and Miles first moved in?"

Her eyes widened. "About then. Although I hadn't thought about it that way."

"Did anything else unusual start around then?"

Again, she shook her head no.

I tried to think of any other questions I could ask. Sunlight through the kitchen window bounced off my spoon and into my eyes. I picked up the spoon and toyed with it, tapping it on the table.

Then a thought hit.

I stood and moved to the kitchen counter, leaving Louise at the table with her coffee.

"Put your hands on the table," I told Louise. "Palms down flat."

She set her cup down and did as I had asked.

I drummed the kitchen counter with my spoon. "Can you feel the vibrations?"

She laughed. "No. You're over there."

"Exactly," I said. I moved back to the table. "Keep your hands where they are."

I banged the spoon on the underside of the table as I spoke. "Now?" I asked. "Can you feel it now?"

"A little," she said, smiling. "Will any of this make sense soon?"

"Well," I told her, "imagine this kitchen table is your land. If someone was digging somewhere else, would you feel the ground shake?"

"No."

"So if someone actually is digging, they would have to be . . ."

" . . . right below," she finished for me. "But that's crazy. Nobody could tunnel beneath my property without my noticing them as they came and went. A bulldozer isn't something you can hide in the trunk of a car."

I grinned. "What if they started a tunnel from somewhere

else and it went under your property? I mean, isn't that the whole point of a tunnel? Going underground where no one notices?"

"This is crazy," she said. "Why would anyone go to that kind of effort?"

"The best way to answer that question is to find where the tunnel starts."

She stared at me for a few minutes and finally realized I was serious.

"I can't let you go looking," she said.

"What can it hurt? Remember, I'm Rocky, the punk loner, the kid no one likes. I'll just go wandering. The worst that can happen is I get kicked off someone's property for trespassing."

"I don't know about this. Your grandfather made it clear you weren't to try anything that could get you in trouble."

"He also gave me a cell phone to use in emergencies," I said. It was strapped to my leg beneath my pants, just as he'd instructed. "Besides, what kind of trouble could I get into in broad daylight?"

CHAPTER 14

An angry bull buffalo with nasty, pointy horns. That's the kind of trouble a person can get into in broad daylight. I discovered that less than an hour after leaving the breakfast table.

Not only was the bull buffalo angry, it was pawing the ground with a massive front hoof and snorting in a way I found extremely discouraging. Especially since it was only half the length of a football field away from me. And with its head lowered, its nasty, pointy horns were aimed directly at my stomach.

A buffalo? Like in a Wild West show? Massive, with a humped back and shaggy, dark brown fur?

I could hardly believe my eyes. Or my ears at the snorting, which grew louder and louder. The only thing that would have surprised me more would have been a dinosaur. *What is a buffalo doing here?*

I had climbed a tall fence to get on this land, just north of Louise Myers' trailer park. The land was mostly grassy, rolling hills. I had been following a rutted trail beside a small creek that wound along the bottom of small hills on each side. It had just occurred to me to wonder what kind of animal made such a deep path in the dirt when, without warning, I'd turned a corner and looked up to see not only this bull buffalo, but also a half dozen cow buffalo.

I wanted to run but could think of no place to go. Behind me were no trees. On each side were no trees. Just the rising hills. The creek to my left was hardly more than a trickle between two shallow banks. There was no way I could dive in and hide underwater.

"Um, nice buffalo?" I tried in a sickly voice.

It snorted and stamped the ground.

I backed up as slowly as I could.

It moved toward me.

I backed up faster.

It snorted and charged!

Sometimes you get so scared that you go beyond panic. It's the type of scared that makes you concentrate so hard on what you have to do that you don't have any room in your mind for fear.

It was closing in with the terrifying speed of a semi truck. I knew I couldn't outrun it. I knew if I turned my back and tried to run, it would trample me in less than a couple of heartbeats.

The only thing I could do was stand still. I'd wait until the last second and pretend to dive one way, but throw myself the other way. It was my only hope.

The buffalo thundered closer and closer.

I tried to keep my weight on the balls of my feet. I pretended the buffalo was a football player moving in to tackle me.

All I needed to do was guess which way to jump and wait as long as possible to do it.

And ...

... the bull buffalo skidded to a stop, its shaggy mane flopping against its sides. It bellowed at me.

In response to its challenge, I gulped loudly back at it. It probably didn't hear, because I noticed it didn't run away.

The buffalo backed up a few steps and began to paw the ground again.

I didn't dare move. That's what had triggered it to charge before.

It bellowed again. But it didn't have a chance to begin another rush, because a black Toyota Land Cruiser, engine roaring, came steaming over the top of the hill above me and to my right. The driver of the four-wheel-drive truck blared the horn and made a beeline for the open land between the buffalo and me.

He jammed on the brakes, and the truck stopped between the buffalo and me. The driver's side of the truck faced me. The passenger side faced the buffalo.

The driver, a lean guy in a cowboy hat, twisted in his seat and reached behind him to pop open the back door of the truck on my side.

"Get in," he shouted. "Sometimes they charge to see if you run. And sometimes they mean it. Not even this truck will help if he gets serious!"

My feet were already moving. I dived into the backseat.

He pulled away before I had a chance to straighten and close the door, fishtailing the vehicle to turn it back up the hill. Long grass scraped against the doorframe. I bounced like a bowling ball on a trampoline as the truck sped over uneven ground. We were halfway to the top of the hill before I finally latched the door shut.

"Thanks," I said. I looked back. The bull buffalo was still below, just turning to go back to the small herd. "I still can't believe it. Buffalo?"

"We breed them here," he said. "And it's private property. What were you doing out there? That bull would have flipped you like you were a hamburger on a grill."

He turned his head slightly. Beneath the cowboy hat, he looked a lot like Joe. A little younger, but the same kind of chin and nose.

"I was just walking around," I said. "I was bored and had nothing to do."

"Walking around?"

"The trailer park," I explained. "I'm forced to stay there with some old lady and—"

"You're the punk my brothers were telling me about," he said. He turned the wheel and guided the truck onto a dirt road. "Some kid with a bad attitude."

"Brothers?"

"Joe and Miles. They live at the trailer court."

"Oh," I said. They hadn't told me their last names. It was news to me that they were brothers. "I met them."

I waited to see if this guy with the cowboy hat would say anything else about Joe and Miles. He didn't. He concentrated on his driving. The road took us past a low, flat building.

"What's that?" I asked.

"An indoor corral," he said. "We run buffalo on this land, in case you hadn't figured that out. We take them in there when they need attention."

"Any other buildings?" I asked. Now that there was a lot of distance between me and the buffalo, I was able to think about other things. Like if there was heavy digging equipment any-where on this land.

"Just that one for buffalo," he grunted.

We reached a gate at the end of the road. He stopped the truck and got out to unlock the chain around the gate. He waved for me to get out of the truck and join him.

When the gate was unlocked, he swung it open and pointed me out.

"Make your own way back from here," he said. "And don't come back. Those buffalo roam anywhere on this land. Next time I might not be around to rescue you."

CHAPTER 15

"They must have moved the buffalo there in the last few months," Louise said when I returned to her mobile home and told her what had happened. "When that land sold a year ago, there was nothing on it."

I was looking at a thick ham sandwich and feeling glad I had all my body parts in place to enjoy eating. "Isn't that unusual?" I asked.

"Buffalo?" she asked.

I nodded.

She shrugged. "Breeding exotic animals is getting to be big business. Some folks have llamas. Others, I've heard, have ostriches. Buffalo aren't that strange. Some farmers breed them with cows to get beefalo."

I bit into the sandwich and wiped mustard off my cheek. It seemed like I had missed something important, and my mind chewed on that as my teeth chewed on the bread.

"Of course," Louise said, pouring us both iced tea, "it is a surprise to me that the new owners decided on running buffalo. I wonder what they had in mind for this place?"

I swallowed. "This place?"

"My trailer park. When they bought that land, they also made me an offer for this. I told them I wasn't interested. My husband had left it to me as a way to support myself, and I wasn't going to sell."

"They? Who are 'they'?"

"I never did find out," Louise said. "At least, not enough to be sure."

The sandwich was halfway to my mouth, but I set it down. This sounded interesting.

"You see, it was a lawyer out of the city of Calgary making the offer. A nice young fellow with a short haircut and a dark blue suit. He wasn't authorized to let me know who he represented. All he ever told me was that he had a client who wanted to buy."

This was getting even more intriguing. I still had the feeling I'd missed something, though.

"Anyhow..." Louise paused as she sipped on her iced tea, "this young lawyer left his briefcase behind and drove off."

She had an embarrassed grin. "I told myself I was looking through it to find his phone number to call him to let him know I had his briefcase. But deep down, I knew I was looking to see if I could find out who his client was. I mean, the lawyer would have come back for his briefcase without my calling. It's just that ... well, it was wrong ... but I snooped."

Adults are a lot easier to like when they admit they're not perfect, and I couldn't help but smile. "Tell me you at least found out."

"Yes," she said. "There was a letter of instruction from a

fellow named David Mellonbee, giving the lawyer permission to act on his behalf."

"And. . . ."

"I found it odd enough to remember, although nearly a year has passed. It was written on letterhead from the Royal Tyrrell Museum."

"The dinosaur museum? Here in Drumheller?"

"Yes. I've often wondered why he was trying to keep his land purchase a secret."

"And now he's breeding buffalo," I said. "You'd think he didn't want people wandering all over the place on—"

I stopped, realizing what I was saying. I repeated myself, speaking faster. "You'd think he didn't want people on his land! Like maybe he was hiding something."

"Well . . ."

It finally dawned on me, the thing that had been nagging at me. It fit with the new owner wanting people to stay off his land. "Did you say all this happened a year ago?"

"Yes, but—"

"And didn't Grandfather John tell me that all the weird stuff started happening here about a year ago?"

"Well, I suppose, but—"

"This might be stretching things," I said. "But what if for some reason this David Mellonbee really, really wanted to buy your trailer park? What if he would do nearly anything to get it? Like arrange for things to happen so that you lose renters? Like make it so bad you can't afford to keep it anymore?"

"That doesn't make sense. It's just a trailer park. Why would he want it?"

"A lot of things don't make sense. Miles and Joe have a

brother who runs the buffalo herd. Miles and Joe have been making things miserable here for you. Dumb as it sounds, someone might be digging beneath the trailer court. And all of this started all around the same time, when someone tried to buy your land and couldn't get it. Not only that, but it was someone who didn't want it publicly known he was buying the land. That alone says something is going on."

I stood and crammed the last piece of sandwich in my mouth.

"You look like you want to go somewhere," she said. She looked amused.

I gulped down the big chunk and followed it with the rest of my iced tea.

"I'll be back in a few hours," I said. "I'm going to be a tourist."

"Tourist?"

"It's time I saw the dinosaur museum, isn't it? Maybe I'll get a chance to speak to someone named David Mellonbee."

CHAPTER 16

Except for the fact I was riding a clunker of a bicycle that had fenders front and back and was at least twenty years old, and except for the fact that I was in heavy black pants and a black T-shirt in hot sunshine, I would have enjoyed my travel. It didn't help that the bike Louise had lent me was hers—a woman's model, of course.

I thought of the public humiliation of getting caught on this bicycle by my friends. Which made me think of my friends. They'd be here tonight. I missed them plenty.

All I had to do was turn my head upward and toward the far side of the valley to see where I would be meeting them at my grandfather's farm. As we had driven to the trailer court the day before, Grandfather John had pointed out where his property stopped at the valley's edge across the river. He had what he called a "full section" of land—640 acres—all planted in wheat. Grandfather John said when he rode his tractor along the edge where the land dropped off, the browns and whites of the Badlands below was one of the prettiest sights he could ever hope to see.

Down here along the river, on the quiet road leading away from Louise's trailer court, it wasn't bad, either. Tall poplars swayed in a slight breeze, the pale underside of leaves fluttering like miniature flags. Occasionally I'd hear a whistle of alarm, and I'd look into the grassy ditch in time to see a small ground squirrel—called a gopher—dive into its burrow. Magpies—black-and-white birds with long tail feathers—bounced from tree to tree, squawking alarm at my passing.

It was so peaceful, I almost forgot I was supposed to be a tough kid who hated the entire world. Until a pickup truck slowed down as it approached.

"Hey," the driver shouted from his open window. "Nice bike. Where's your skirt?"

The guy didn't look much older than me. Probably just got his driver's license. The passenger in the truck, even younger looking, laughed at his friend's question.

Normally, I would have made a joke, tried to get all of us laughing together. After all, it was a stupid woman's bike, and I'm sure I looked dumb. But I was Rocky, with scruffy black hair and an earring.

I stopped and got off the bicycle. I dropped it on the road and walked toward the truck. Inside, I was pretending to be a kid capable of burning down a mobile home.

"Look, you pimple-faced wimp," I said, dead serious, stopping to stand with my legs apart and my arms crossed, "there's a reason I ride that bike."

The driver shrank back a bit, slightly nervous at my lack of fear. "What's the reason?"

"Because I can. And I'm tough enough to do something

about it if people want to give me grief."

"Oh," he said. He glanced over at his friend. His friend shrugged. He looked back at me with a hesitant smile. His eyes took in my bad haircut and my clothes. "That's a real good reason."

He drove away in a hurry.

This scared me, how it had become so easy to pretend to be someone else. Was I enjoying being Rocky a little too much?

I got back on my bike and pedaled toward the world-famous Royal Tyrrell Museum. It took another half hour. I hopped off and locked the bike against a pillar. Cars and mini-vans cruised past, filled with moms and dads and kids pressing their faces against the window to stare at the statues of dinosaurs on the entry plaza to the museum.

The full-size monsters stared back from their frozen positions in front of the museum. A fountain among them added to the scene. On the other side of the road was a hill with stairs to climb to a viewing point of the eerie Badlands stretching to the valley hills.

For about the hundredth time, I wished my friends were here with me to look around. Things are definitely more fun when they are shared.

But I was alone.

I walked toward the museum entrance. Somewhere inside, if it worked out right, I'd find a man named David Mellonbee. More important, I needed to find out as much as possible *about* him.

CHAPTER 17

All I could think was . . . cool. Very cool.

Although there were hundreds of people, the inside of the museum felt still and hushed, probably because everyone else was just as fascinated as I was. I began to roam, my eyes open wide. There was plenty to see. The museum was broken into large chambers, so it was like stepping through time. I walked slowly, soaking it in. From the triceratops with its long horns, to the dromiceiomimus skeleton guarding fossilized eggs, to the Jurassic killer allosaurus biting down on a helpless camptosaurus. Some of the dinosaurs were left as skeletons, others were fleshed out and terrifying. It didn't matter to me that I couldn't pronounce any of the names; I enjoyed it so much I delayed asking about Mellonbee to keep looking.

It took me nearly two hours to get to every exhibit because the museum wasn't just dinosaurs taken from the Badlands around us. There was an Ice Age exhibit, an underwater exhibit, and my favorite, the Gigantic Insects display. Some of them were as big as hawks, and I squirmed to think of mosquitoes that big.

The exhibit that caught me most and stunned all the people around it into low tones of awe was the king tyrant lizard—tyrannosaurus rex. This monstrous skeleton had been discovered along the Red Deer River north of the museum. Just standing below it, I was frightened. Its skull was higher than I was tall. I paced out fourteen steps from its tail to its nose. I shuddered to think about being tossed around in its jaws like a rat in the mouth of a wolfhound.

As I stood there, I began to think about what my dad had told me about the Bible. He'd started the talk because of Joel, who had asked him why dinosaurs weren't mentioned in the Bible.

At Joel's question, Dad had smiled. He'd started by telling us he welcomed difficult questions because God was truth, and truth could stand up to any questions. He'd said sometimes there would be questions that no man could answer because God's universe was a wonderful place of mystery; the more answers scientists found about it, the more questions they came up with, but unsolvable mysteries didn't mean a person should stop asking questions.

Dad told us to think of humans as spiders crawling around the basement of a house and doing their own scientific tests on the house. The spiders might actually be able to come up with theories on how the house worked—electrical wiring, furnace vents, water pipes, just like scientists were finding out more and more about how the universe worked, from subatomic levels to the physics of the galaxies. Yet, those spiders still would have to account somehow for the builder of the house; it couldn't just appear from nowhere. In the same way, we should look beyond the universe for its creator.

For example, Dad had said, scientists have discovered the rate of expansion of the universe. If it had expanded fractionally faster, gravity wouldn't be able to hold things together. If it had expanded fractionally more slowly, it would have collapsed back in on itself. Many scientists, he said, were beginning to realize that such a perfect rate of expansion could not be coincidence.

What really stuck with me was that Dad had told Joel and me that the Bible was not a book of how, but a book of why. The Bible wasn't intended as a manual to answer scientific questions, but it was a map God gave for helping us understand the why of life and the decisions we needed to make as we went through life. *"What was more important,"* Dad had asked us in return, *"how God had created the world, or why?"*

There was a question, I thought, looking at the T. rex. Why dinosaurs? I made a mental note to zing Dad with that one when I got back to Jamesville.

But I had other questions, of course. Namely, a name. David Mellonbee.

I went back to the entrance to the museum.

I found a lady with a museum badge. She was an older lady, short, and had to look up to me with her kind brown eyes.

"Ma'am," I said, "have you heard of someone named David Mellonbee?"

"Of course," she said. "Dr. Mellonbee is our chief paleontologist."

Chief paleontologist.

There must have been a puzzled frown on my face because she smiled and continued, "That's the study of fossils."

"Thank you," I said, as if I needed someone to tell me this

museum was about fossils. "Is he working here now?"

"I'm afraid not," she said. "Although we do have a section of the museum where you can view the prep lab and see what paleontologists do."

"Thank you," I said. There was only one paleontologist I wanted to see, even from a distance. "You mean David . . . Dr. Mellonbee doesn't work for the museum any longer?"

"Oh, dear. Just the opposite. He's a world expert. We're delighted to have him as part of our expert staff."

"So he is here?"

"No."

She was so sweet, I couldn't get mad. Still, it was frustrating. "He's on your staff but he doesn't work here?"

A little boy in a blue T-shirt ran up to her and tugged on her skirt. She looked down.

"Where's the bathroom?" he asked in a panic-filled voice, hopping from leg to leg.

She pointed. He ran in that direction, but I was pretty sure it was too late. It was impossible to miss the shiny track he left as he ran.

"Oh dear," she said. "I'll need to call for a cleanup."

"Yes, ma'am," I said. "Um, Dr. Mellonbee, where would I find him?"

"Oh yes, that's what you meant. He's finishing things at the Chrisman dig."

"Dig?"

"Tyrannosaurus rex. They're uncovering the most complete skeleton ever found in the world. It's worth millions."

"Millions?"

"Millions. Now, where can I find someone to clean up this mess?"

She scurried away from me. Her concern was a little easier to solve than mine.

Millions. I had no idea what all this meant, but somehow it had to be connected to the problem at the trailer court.

A lady in a yellow cotton dress moved closer as she called in a nervous voice, "Bobby? Bobby?"

She looked so worried I interrupted. "Is Bobby a blond kid with a blue T-shirt and shorts?"

The lady frowned at my earring and black pants and black shirt.

"Yes," she said with suspicion. "What about him?"

I pointed at the shiny wet puddle trail. "Follow that, ma'am. You should find him no problem."

Even guys like Rocky do good deeds once in a while.

CHAPTER 18

"Phone's for you," Louise said. Her face was puzzled. "Some guy speaking half Spanish."

That would be Mike Andrews. He liked trying out different accents on strangers. I was tempted to suggest I'd call back later. On the supper table in front of me was a stack of hamburgers a foot high, and it was my goal to lovingly squeeze every single one into my stomach. It had been a long afternoon at the museum and a long ride back.

"Thanks," I said, standing from the table. "And thanks for the burgers."

She smiled. "You do pack food away."

I put the telephone to my ear.

"Señor? You pack eet away? What ees eet you pack away?"

"Hey, Mike. What's up?"

"Up?" he said. "What do you mean, what's up? We're at your grandfather's farm. Remember? Vacation?"

"Yeah," I said. I mean, much as I missed them, a guy has to be cool. "I think I'll be down here for a few more days."

Louise had talked to Grandfather John about it. It seemed like a good idea to wait until I knew what diversion Miles and Joe wanted.

"A few days? But—"

His voice rose as someone grabbed the phone from him.

"Ricky?"

"Hi, Lisa," I said. If there was one girl I kind of liked for serious, it was Lisa Higgins. She had long dark hair and a smile that could melt diamonds in a freezer. Not only that, but she was smart and had a great baseball arm. She had been hanging around with Mike and Ralphy and me for years.

"Miss us?" she asked.

"Hmmph," I said.

"That's what I thought. I miss you, too."

I hoped Louise didn't notice that my ears were turning red.

"Here's Ralphy," she said.

There was a slight pause.

"Hey, hey, hey," he said quickly. Ralphy's our computer nut. Hair that stands out in all directions and baggy loose shirts that never stay tucked in his pants. If RAM and ROM and keyboards were part of the Olympics, he'd have gold medals in every event.

"How's life?" I asked.

"Cool, except for your brother."

I groaned. "Big surprise. What's he doing now?"

"He liked the idea you and Mike had for trying to win money with a home video. And your mom made the mistake of allowing us to take along your family's camcorder. So ever since we got off the airplane in Calgary, he's had it stuck to his eyeball. While I was changing here at your grandfather's, he managed to get this one shot of me in my boxers, and already he's shown it to Lisa a dozen times."

"Poor girl," I said.

"Her? What about me? It's no fun that—"

"Ask my grandfather if you guys can visit here tonight. I've got some things to tell you and a favor to ask."

I wanted to see if they could go to the dinosaur excavation tomorrow and find out if David Mellonbee was doing anything unusual there.

"Sure," Ralphy said. "He's outside right now. I'll ask him to call you right back."

Grandfather John did call right back, but in the minute while I was waiting I still managed to eat a hamburger and a half.

"I need to go into town anyway," he said in answer to my question. "I'll drop your friends off in about an hour. Let me suggest that you do your visiting inside Louise's home. No one has to know that you all are friends. And in a day or two, you can move back up to the farm and enjoy the rest of your vacation, just like it was first planned."

The hour went quickly. I finished the burgers and helped Louise with dishes. When the doorbell rang, I hurried to answer it. It would be good to see them again.

I opened the door to see their familiar faces. Ralphy, short and skinny, stood in front of Mike. Lisa stood beside both of them.

"Yikes," Mike said. He stepped back to look at the house number. "Do we have the right address?"

"Guys," I said. "Come on in."

Lisa stepped forward and stared into my face. "Ricky?"

Mike and Ralphy began to bust out laughing.

"Oh," I said. "I guess Grandfather John hasn't told you much, has he?"

CHAPTER 19

Louise brought everyone inside to the kitchen, where we sat around the table, Ralphy and Mike on one side, Lisa and I on the other side. Louise scooped ice cream into bowls, poured fudge sauce and nuts on the ice cream, and set the bowls down in front of us.

"If you want more," she said, "just holler."

She began to walk toward the living room area.

"Why don't you join us?" Lisa asked Louise.

When Louise turned around, the smile on her face told me that Lisa's invitation had been something Louise liked. I understood at that moment that life might sometimes be lonely for someone like Louise. Without her husband, she probably had a lot of sadness, no matter how cheerful she might appear to the rest of the world.

"I'm not sure," Louise said. "You young people need time by yourselves...."

"Why don't you sit down," I said. I stood and bee-lined for the refrigerator. "Do you want fudge sauce on your ice cream?"

Louise took the chair at the end of the table. While

I was getting her a bowl of ice cream, Mike whispered something and Ralphy started laughing. I turned around and glared at them. I knew exactly why they were laughing. At my hair and my clothes.

"Shut your mouths," I snarled. "Or I'll rip your eyeballs out and stuff them up your nostrils."

It stopped them in a big hurry. Ralphy's jaw almost fell into his ice cream.

I grinned. "Pretty good, huh? That's me as Rocky, all-around jerk and juvenile delinquent. Let me tell you about it."

It took fifteen minutes to catch them up on everything—my first afternoon here, meeting Miles and Joe, trying to burn down a mobile home, getting chased by a buffalo, my trip to the Royal Tyrrell Museum, and some of my questions about all of this.

When I finished, Mike whistled. "So you think someone is doing some heavy digging around here."

"Crazy as it sounds, the answer is yes. I felt the ground shaking. Louise says it has happened a lot of times. Miles and Joe said they need a diversion soon to cover some even bigger digging."

"Like someone is mining underneath us?" Ralphy asked.

"It's all I can figure," I said.

"I don't get it," Mike said. "If someone is making a mine below the trailer park, why would they want to buy the trailer park? I mean, once they get what they're looking for, they don't need to own it."

"Good point," I said. "Believe me, there are more questions than answers. And what's the connection with all of this to

David Mellonbee at the museum? Why was he trying to buy this without anyone knowing?"

Lisa was drumming the table with her fingers. She stopped suddenly. "Ricky, I don't mean to change the subject, but don't you think it was strange that the guy appeared in the SUV at exactly the right time to rescue you from the buffalo?"

"I was praying like crazy," I said. "God was listening."

Louise smiled at my profound theology.

"Maybe God decided to help in another way, too," Lisa replied with her own—very pretty—smile.

"Meaning?" I asked her.

"You just told us that you wondered if the buffalo were on that property to keep people from wandering around."

I nodded. That had been part of my fifteen minutes of explaining.

"If you were worried about people on your property," she continued, "wouldn't you also find other ways to make it secure?"

Ralphy broke in. His nose was dabbed with ice cream. "They could monitor the property in a lot of ways! Video cameras! Heat sensors! Motion detectors! Sure! Lisa's right. They probably knew you were there the entire time!"

Lisa reached over with a napkin and wiped the ice cream off Ralphy's nose. "Which means," she said, "if you're thinking of going back there to look around, you have to be careful."

How could she be so accurate in reading my mind?

"If you guys are right," Louise said, "somebody is going to a lot of trouble and spending a lot of money, and the big question is still *why*. Mike's right, too. Why buy the property if you've already dug out what you wanted?"

There was silence around the table as we all wondered.

"What next?" Ralphy asked to finally break the silence. "If any of these crazy theories are actually true, what do we do next? Call the police?"

"Not police. Mounties. Royal Canadian Mounted Police." I grinned. "I've been learning about Canada. They have these neat ceremonial horse rides. A tradition from when they were mounted police a hundred years ago in the Wild West out here."

"Mounties," Ralphy repeated. "Call them?"

"Not yet. They'd think we were crazy. I was hoping you guys might want to do something for me tomorrow."

"Like what?" Mike asked. He had his hat on backward and gave me a suspicious look.

"Not much," I said. "At least if you consider checking out a dinosaur excavation not much."

"Dinosaur excavation?" Louise said.

I nodded yes. "What if David Mellonbee is the key to all of this? At the museum, they told me he is spending most of his days at a new dinosaur find. Everyone's excited about it because they think it will be the most complete fossilized tyrannosaurus rex ever found in the world."

"Sure," Louise said. "Although I've heard the dig is nearly finished, it was big news a few summers back. All over the newspapers and television. A big oil company was trenching around a drill site on Fred Chrisman's land, and one of the bulldozer men noticed a huge bone. They stopped bulldozing and called the museum."

"Sorry to interrupt," I said. "Oil company? Fred Chrisman? You sound like you know a lot about this."

"This is a small community," Louise answered. "News like this, most people know about it. Chrisman's a farmer a few miles up the valley. On the other side of the river. What happened was an oil company went in to drill a well. . . ."

"They can just do that?" Ralphy asked. "Drill anywhere they want?"

"Not quite," Louise told him, a hint of a smile on her face. "From what I understand, the oil company does geological surveys and tries to decide the most likely place to find oil. Then they approach the farmer and make a deal with him, offering him a certain amount of money to let them drill. If they find oil, they have to pay him more. They pay royalties if the land's been in the family long enough that they own the oil rights. The more oil, the more money the farmer makes."

"So this Chrisman guy can become a millionaire?" I asked.

"Sometimes," she said. "Not all oil wells produce oil. And in this case, they had to stop drilling."

"Because of the discovery of the dinosaur," Lisa said.

"Exactly."

"The farmer must be upset," I said. "Having a chance at all that oil money and then getting it taken away because of some old bones."

"Folks tell me that Fred Chrisman didn't mind that much. He's close to retiring and is well off anyway. From what I hear, he's happy to help out. It's the Royal Tyrrell Museum that benefits the most. There's no other place in the world that will have this new dinosaur find. Besides, Fred would get some government compensation for this."

"Lots of money?" Mike asked.

"Probably," Louise said. "But Fred Chrisman decided to

donate the T. rex to the museum. Do you guys really think that has anything to do with any of this?"

"If it doesn't," I said, "trying to find out is still more interesting than boring summer days back home."

I looked around the table at my friends. "Right, guys?"

"Right," they said together.

"We'll look around tomorrow," Lisa said. "We'll see what we can find out about the excavation on the Chrisman property. And, Ricky, what will you do?"

"Be Rocky," I said. "I'll go around this trailer park getting people to hate me more and more. Hopefully, I'll learn more from Miles and Joe."

"But we can't forget the most important thing of all," Mike added.

We waited for him to continue.

"All my ice cream is gone," he said. "And remember, Louise, you said just holler if we wanted more?"

CHAPTER 20

Miles and Joe found me at noon the next day. I was hanging out in front of Louise's store, being a jerk and sitting on the steps where people had to walk around me, reading comic books. They drove up in their green pickup truck and parked directly in front of the store.

"Look," Joe said to Miles as they stepped out of the truck. "The kid's wearing a red shirt. He actually has something else besides black."

"Better than not changing shirts," I said. "Not naming names. Joe."

"And he can read without moving his lips," Joe said as a return insult.

"You must have seen me reading from far away," I told him.

"Huh?"

"Because it would take someone as dumb as you a long time to come up with that line."

"Kid, just once . . ."

"Settle down, you two," Miles said. "And let's move out of here."

I followed both of them to their pickup truck.

"Get in," Miles said.

I didn't really want to. It meant having to sit between Miles and Joe. Tough as I liked to sound, Joe made me very nervous.

"Where are we going?" I asked.

"Shut up," Joe said. "You'll see when we get there."

Squished between the two of them, I was thankful it wasn't a long drive. The worst part of it was Joe's body odor. I wanted to ask him if he knew how to spell *soap* but decided I'd be wiser to wait until I had room to run.

After leaving the trailer park, Miles turned a sharp left toward the land with the herd of buffalo. He left the road and drove the truck down a dirt path which followed the fence along the property. I was glad the buffalo were on the other side of the fence; if it came to a head-butting contest between the buffalo and this old truck, the truck would lose.

Miles stopped a few minutes down the dirt road.

"Out," he said as he clicked the ignition off.

Joe and I got out. I was glad for fresh air. Opposite the truck, on the other side of the fence, was a small bulldozer. Miles pointed at it.

"Want to have some fun and get paid for it?" he asked.

"As much fun as getting caught by a security guard you guys never told me about?"

"For the last time," Joe nearly shouted, "we never knew about him. If you shove that in our faces again, I'm going to—"

"Joe . . ." Miles's voice was weary. "Haven't you figured out you can't scare this kid with threats?"

Miles didn't know how wrong he was. I didn't, however, correct him.

Miles turned to me. "Remember that grand, kid."

"One thousand dollars?" It was easy to sound like I didn't believe him, mainly because I didn't.

"Yup," he said, "like I told you before, one thousand dollars. Not only that, you get free driving lessons. Climb the fence."

"This fence? But—" I stopped myself. I was about to tell them I was worried about a buffalo herd that might be anywhere. Rocky, though, wouldn't show that he cared.

"But what?"

"But I haven't seen any money." It was the only thing I could think of on short notice.

Miles grinned a wolf grin. "I like you, kid."

He pulled a roll of hundred-dollar bills out of his pocket and counted five of them. He slapped them into my hand.

"Half now," he said. "Half when you finish the job. Are you satisfied?"

Could I say no? Especially with the money now bulging from my front pocket? Especially when I needed to find out what they intended?

"Satisfied," I said. "Once I learn how to drive the bulldozer, what next?"

"Tonight," he said, "you bust it through the fence."

Miles pointed over my shoulder, back toward the trailer park. "See, it's not that far as the crow flies to all those mobile homes. At exactly midnight, you're going to take that bulldozer straight across and rip through as many trailers as you can before you have to jump and run."

Miles looked at Joe and grinned an even bigger wolf grin. "Between that and the buffalo running loose from the hole in the fence, no one will have time to worry about the real action."

"What's that?" I asked. I tried not to blink or show any expression. I didn't want them to realize how badly I wanted to know what they intended.

Miles and Joe both froze and stared at me.

Had I pushed too far?

"Mind your own business," Joe said. "Snoopy noses sometimes get cut off."

I shrugged, like I didn't care.

They kept staring at me. With a chill, I understood that it wouldn't bother them at all to cut off my nose. Or worse.

"Hey," I said, knowing this was the time I most needed to sound tough, "if you two have a problem with a simple question, you can take your money back and use it to blow your noses."

"Relax." Miles finally grinned, a gleaming of white in the middle of his bushy beard. "You're just the kid we need."

But in the next moment his face darkened, and I felt the ice of his eyes. "Still," he said, "for your own health, make sure it stays that way."

CHAPTER 21

Six hours later, in the kitchen, I stood when the phone rang.

"I'll get it," I told Louise. "It's probably Mike. He said he'd call around now and tell me what they learned today at the dinosaur excavation."

Only it wasn't Mike.

"Richard?"

"Yes," I said, suddenly nervous. It was Grandfather John. Why had he spoken so softly? Why had he called me Richard?

"Richard, please tell me that your brother and your friends are with you."

"I can't," I said into the telephone, even more nervous. "I didn't know they were supposed to be here."

"They weren't," he said. "I was just hoping."

"Hoping?"

"I haven't seen them or heard from them since they went to Fred Chrisman's land. I thought maybe they'd taken their bicycles and ridden down to the trailer park."

"They probably went exploring," I said. "Mike's

like that. He doesn't have much of an attention span."

"Lisa promised to have all of them back by now," he told me.

This was different. Lisa was as steady as Mike was unpredictable.

"Um, maybe they took the wrong turn."

"No," he said. "Fred Chrisman's farm is just down the valley from where I live. That's why I let them go by themselves."

Louise moved in front of me. She frowned with worry. I guessed she'd heard enough of my end of the conversation to know something was wrong. I smiled at her with assurance I didn't feel.

"I can't believe anything serious has happened," I said. This was Canada. People here were polite and nice. Crime was something that happened in New York and Los Angeles.

"There's no need to panic. I didn't say anything had happened to them," Grandfather John told me. Although his tone of voice had said plenty. "I'm just concerned. I've been up and down the road several times, and I've seen no sign of them."

I was more than concerned. By now, I had no doubt Joe and Miles were mean and able to seriously hurt people. If Joe and Miles were connected to David Mellonbee and the excavation, and if somehow they had discovered Mike and Ralphy and Lisa and Joel were spying . . .

Louise motioned for me to give her the phone.

"John," she began, "what's wrong?"

She listened, frowning even more.

"Call the police?" she finally asked. She tilted the phone, inviting me to listen. I brought my head close to hers and strained to hear my grandfather's reply.

"Not yet," he said. His voice was faint; Louise held the phone a little from her ear so that I could hear better. "I'll give them another hour or so. I mean, there's no reason to think anything but the fact that some kids are late for their evening meal. It happens all the time, right?"

"Right," Louise said. "Does this change the plans you and Ricky made for tonight?"

Earlier in the afternoon I'd called Grandfather John and told him that Miles and Joe wanted me to do some major bull-dozing. We had decided what to do about it, and all I had left was the wait until he met me at the bulldozer around midnight.

"Things will change only if his brother and friends don't show up," he said. "See if you can get Richard to grab a nap beforehand."

"Sure," she said. "I'll call if they show up here. And you call me the instant you see them. I don't want to worry the entire night."

"Deal," he said. "Good night."

There was a click and a dial tone. Slowly she set the phone on its cradle.

"Nothing to worry about," she said.

When grown-ups tell you there's nothing to worry about, there's always a reason. Like there is something to worry about.

"Sure," I said. "Would you like help with the dishes?"

"Don't worry about them. Why don't you go for a walk along the river or something. There's lots of daylight left, and I think boys your age need plenty of fresh air."

I took her advice. Which was a mistake.

A half hour later, Miles and Joe found me at the riverbank. Joe was carrying a rifle. He pointed the barrel at my stomach and told me to put my hands above my head.

CHAPTER 22

"Very funny," I said, although my mouth was so dry with fear I could hardly speak.

"Do it," Miles commanded. "And drop the attitude."

Of the two, Miles was the one who liked me. If he was mad, this was serious. But I had no idea why.

I put my hands on my head.

Joe gave the rifle to Miles. Miles held it steady at my chest. The black hole of the barrel seemed as big as a dinner plate. I expected a belch of flame at any second, then realized if he pulled the trigger I'd be dead long before my eyes saw anything or my ears heard anything.

"You were easy to follow," Miles said. "Once we knew you were headed to the river, Joe went back and got the truck."

"Truck?"

"You'll see," Miles said. "Later. But first we have a little test we want to run on you. If you pass, we owe you an apology. If not . . ."

Joe moved close and cuffed me across the head. "I've been dying to do that," he said. "Now, move down to the river and lay on your stomach."

I hesitated.

He cuffed me again and pushed me toward the water. I got on my knees on a thin bar of gravel along the bank.

"Face up to the water," he said.

I lay down on my chest. Some water seeped into my shirt. The cold was a shock.

"Crawl forward," Miles said.

I moved ahead until my elbows were in the flowing water.

"Crawl forward," Miles repeated.

I moved until my upper body was in the river. The water sucked at me, and I had to push with my arms to keep my face out of the water.

Joe, right behind me, grabbed my hair at the back of my head.

"Dunk," Miles said from where he stood on the riverbank.

"Huh?" I said.

"Dunk. Or Joe will do it for you."

I still didn't understand.

Joe pushed on my head and kept me under so long I thought he meant to drown me. I got my first real understanding of his strength, because as much as I flailed and kicked, I could not reach air. He seemed like a solid rock. And still he would not let me up.

Just at the point I thought I would inhale a lungful of water, he pulled my head out. I sputtered and gasped for air.

He pushed me down again. And kept me under for another eternity.

He pulled my head up into the sweet air, and I drew in new life.

"Enough," Miles barked to Joe. "His hair's wet."

Joe rubbed my head. He held his palm open in front of my face. Black dye streamed off his skin with the river water that dripped from his hand.

Black dye. As in black dye from my hair. They'd forced me into the river not to drown me, but to wash the dye from my hair. *How did they find out?*

Joe grabbed my belt and pulled me to my feet. They both understood the look on my face.

"You got it, kid," Miles said. "You're pretending to be someone you're not. We're wondering why you're playing this scam on us."

"You've got a lot of explaining to do," Joe added from behind my back. "And let me tell you, I'm real happy about the possibility of getting you to talk the hard way if you don't explain."

Joe shoved me back to the riverbank. As I stumbled to keep my balance, Miles switched the rifle to a one-handed grip, and with his free hand, he reached into his shirt pocket. He came out with a long strip of black cloth, which he tossed to Joe.

Miles brought the rifle up to my chest level and pointed it. "He'll talk, Joe. Not here. We'll put him with the others. He can talk there. Then Mellonbee can decide what to do."

Others? Mellonbee?

"But I'd really like to hurt him now," Joe said.

"And if someone happens to stop by?" Miles asked. "We'll move him first. You got the blindfold. You know what to do with it."

"All right, all right." Joe sounded disappointed. He moved beside me, reached above my head, and slid the black cloth over my eyes. He knotted the blindfold so tight I wondered if my skull would pop.

"Tape his hands with that roll I already gave you," Miles said. "And carry him. It's not far to the truck."

Joe wrapped my wrists together with twenty rounds of tape. He lifted me without even a grunt and laid me over his shoulders like I was no more than a big bag of puffed wheat.

He walked for hardly more than five minutes. In that time, Joe managed to swing me into every tree and brush along the path. I doubted it was an accident.

Totally blind, I had no warning when we reached the truck. When he dropped me, I yelped, expecting to hit the ground. Instead, I thumped down only a few inches. It felt like I was in the back of the truck.

One door clicked open, then slammed shut. The next door did the same. The engine started and the truck lurched forward.

There I was, a helpless pigeon between two wolves. Two questions were the biggest in my mind. Where was the wolves' den? And what did they intend to do when we got there?

CHAPTER 23

I did my best to keep track of the truck's motion. For the first while—I counted to 300—it traveled slowly, rocking and bumping, with branches scraping on both sides. I guessed, then, that for five minutes we had driven down a narrow dirt road through trees.

Then, briefly, the tires hummed and wind whipped my hair. A paved road?

The truck slowed and turned. I had no idea of direction. Gravel sprayed as it picked up speed. Almost immediately, however, it slowed again, then stopped.

The door on the passenger side clicked open. The truck bounced a little as someone stepped out. Seconds later there came a creaking sound. I tried to place the noise, but I couldn't make sense of it.

The truck moved ahead without the passenger— probably Joe—getting inside. That confused me, until the truck stopped almost immediately.

Creaking again. Then more bouncing as someone stepped back into the truck. The slam of the passenger door.

I realized then that the driver had stopped for the

passenger to open a gate, had driven through, then stopped for the passenger to shut the gate and get back inside.

The truck shifted from low gear to the next. I had reached only two hundred in my counting this time before it slowed and turned hard. It traveled a few seconds more, then stopped.

The passenger door opened again. There was a hollow echo—as if a big steel garage door had been lifted. The truck drove ahead. Although my eyes were blindfolded, I instantly knew we'd driven into darkness—a large building?—for my skin cooled immediately.

The passenger door slammed shut again, and the truck rolled forward.

I started counting again.

The truck rolled so slowly that I felt no breeze across my wet skin and clothing. Yet it was not on a bumpy road. I wondered why the driver had decided to keep it so slow.

Was it my imagination? The air seemed to grow cooler.

Finally the truck stopped. Both doors clanged open and then shut.

Strong hands yanked me from the truck bed and dragged me over the side. I barely managed to get my feet beneath me before I was dropped.

Click.

It was the switchblade Joe had pulled on me a night earlier!

Cold steel did not, as I expected, slice into my skin. Joe slipped the blade between my blindfold and my face and cut through the cloth. The blindfold fell away.

"Guys?" I said in disbelief. Straight ahead were my friends, Mike, Lisa, Ralphy, and my brother, Joel. Joel had his teddy bear with him. Normally that would make me smile. But not now.

"Sorry," Mike said. "We didn't mean to get you in all this trouble."

I stared at all of them. Their wrists and ankles were taped, and they were sitting on a dirt floor, leaning against a dirt wall.

Bare bulbs dangled from crossbeams above us, giving a harsh light. From what I could tell, we were at the end of a tunnel barely wider than the truck behind me. The tunnel walls and ceiling were braced by sturdy beams of wood.

"What's going on?" I asked, more to them than Joe and Miles.

Joe slammed his palm against my head. "You obviously don't understand. We're the ones asking you what's going on. And if your answers don't match the ones we already got from your friends, all of you are going to get hurt a lot, a little at a time."

He grinned and his teeth gleamed. "We'll start by hurting the girl first, then move on to your brother."

If they knew Joel was my brother, they probably knew most of it anyway. So I told Miles and Joe everything.

When I finished, they looked at each other.

"What do you think?" Joe asked Miles.

"I think it's time for Dave to make a decision."

Joe nodded. "Want me to stay behind and guard them?"

"Nah," Miles said. "Just tape his ankles and throw him among the others. That will hold them until we get back."

Joe toppled me onto my side and wrapped my ankles with as much enthusiasm as he had done on my wrists. I knew it would take ten minutes with a sharp knife to cut me loose.

Which was not good news. We didn't have a sharp knife.

Joe rolled me toward my friends. Miles was already in the truck.

Joe hopped inside.

The truck began to back up, then it stopped. Joe rolled down his window.

"Go ahead and scream your brains out," Joe said. "It's five hundred yards of tunnel to the surface. You could play a rock concert down here and no one would know."

He rolled his window up, and the truck rolled away from us. Its headlights grew smaller and smaller and remained visible for minutes until finally disappearing.

"Well," I said, "anyone know any good campfire songs?"

CHAPTER 24

"It was the middle of the afternoon, and we were watching from a hill just above the dinosaur excavation," Mike explained. "There wasn't much to see, actually. Just three guys standing around poking at dirt. We were almost ready to go back and—"

"It wasn't my fault," Ralphy interrupted. "A bee landed on my shoulder. I was trying to shake it loose and—"

"The short story is that Ralphy slipped and fell," Lisa said. "You know how the sides of these hills are that smooth, white dry clay?"

"Nothing to stop me," Ralphy confirmed. "I slid all the way down. They made Mike and Lisa and Joel come down, too."

"Those two guys," Joel said quietly. "Mean. Ugly. Took my camcorder."

"Camcorder?" I said.

For a few moments, no one answered my question. I took a closer look around. My eyes were adjusting to the darkness beyond the light bulbs, and I saw that we were not—as I had first assumed—at the end of the tunnel. Beyond us—in the opposite direction from where the truck had left—the tunnel widened. All I could see from where I sat was a deeper blackness.

The tunnel walls themselves had deep grooves in the dirt. My guess was the grooves came from the giant teeth of the huge steel bucket of an excavating machine. All of this confirmed what we had decided earlier. Someone had been digging deep in the ground. Were we below the trailer court right now?

"Camcorder," Mike finally said. "We didn't think there would be any harm in taking Joel. Joel, of course, wanted to take the camcorder."

"My idea," Lisa said. "I thought it would look innocent if there was a kid with us. And it would have worked, except..."

"You should have seen the two guys," Ralphy said. "They went crazy! Threw us all in the trunk of this big old Cadillac and—"

"Whoa," I said. "Back up. Which two guys?"

"Mean. Ugly," Joel repeated. "Those two."

"The two guys who drove you here in the truck," Mike said. "You know. One with a ball cap and arms as big as elephant legs. The other with a beard and looks like a hillbilly."

"Joe and Miles. The two guys from the trailer court."

"So there definitely is a connection between the trailer court stuff and the dinosaur dig," Lisa said.

"Great." This came from Mike. He lifted his taped wrists. "Now that we know, let's just bite through this tape and find a way to arrest them. Of course, since we were in the trunk of the car all the way here, we have no idea where we are, but let's not let a detail like that stop us."

"Camcorder, guys." I ignored his sarcasm. "What happened

with the camcorder? Why did that get you in trouble?"

More silence.

"Guys?"

"They played back the videotape," Ralphy admitted. "You know how you can rewind it and look in the viewfinder to see what you've taped? They wanted to know why we had the video camera and what we were filming."

"Yeah. And . . ." I couldn't understand why they looked so guilty.

"They rewound it to the beginning," Mike said. "While we were standing there, trying to explain we were just tourists."

"And . . ."

"It was a videotape from home," Lisa explained. "The first five minutes showed Joel and your mom and dad and you."

"An innocent family," I said. "Why would that get you in all this trouble?"

"It got you in this trouble, too," Ralphy said. "I'm really sorry, pal. I should have let that bee crawl into my shirt if it wanted."

"Me in trouble?"

"They went crazy," Lisa said. "The guy with the tattoos on his arms. He looked at you on the videotape and started yelling about Rocky with blond hair and what was going on."

I understood. They'd seen me as Ricky. Joel's camcorder had blown my cover as Rocky the punk. They'd instantly known that Mike and Ralphy and Lisa and Joel were somehow part of what I was doing in disguise. Which is why they'd followed me from the trailer park until I was alone at the river. Which is why they dunked my head in the water to check the true color of my hair.

"This is not good," I said.

Their miserable silence gave total agreement.

I struggled to my feet. It was tough to stay upright with my feet taped together and my hands bound in front of me.

"What's over there?" I asked, motioning my head at the blackness where the tunnel widened.

"Haven't looked," Mike said. "We can barely move."

Neither could I. But this made so little sense I didn't care. I hopped and fell, got up, hopped and fell, got up, hopped and fell. It took about five minutes. I managed to get to where the tunnel walls widened. It took another few minutes to make sense of what I saw in the dimness.

"Bones," I called back to the guys. "Big bones. Huge, huge bones. Lying in soft dirt."

I pictured the biggest dinosaur skeleton I had seen in the Royal Tyrrell Museum.

"Maybe it's a tyrannosaurus rex," I said, still calling back to them. "But I don't get it. How did they know to dig right to this spot?"

"Um, Ricky?"

"Yeah, Mike?" I stared into the dimness without looking back at him. I could hardly make out the details of the bones. They looked scattered in no particular order. The dirt almost covered all of the bones. Had someone just started to dig around them?

"We've got company," Mike said, his voice grim, almost choked.

"Huh?" I snapped my head back toward the light bulbs above them.

"Yes, my troublesome friend," a strange man said, standing

beside my friends. "My name is David Mellonbee. Perhaps you recall asking around about me? I've just come down the tunnel on a little stroll. Please, do come and join us. I'll tell you about the tyrant of the Badlands. And why you are going to die because of it."

CHAPTER 25

David Mellonbee was tall and thin. He wore khaki trousers and a neatly pressed polo shirt. His light blond hair was combed over to one side and slicked down, like he was trying to cover a bald patch.

As I hopped closer, he watched me like a cat eyeing a crippled bird. He smiled, with his left hand stroking a thick goatee much darker than the hair on his head.

"Your guess was most astute," he said. "Tyrannosaurus rex. The king tyrant lizard. Think of a double-decker bus on two legs, running faster than a deer. Alive, it could swallow you in two bites. A single one of its teeth is the size of a banana. A most fascinating creature."

He paused. "When people think of dinosaurs, they think of T. rex. Horrible, gruesome, completely fascinating. And only about two dozen have been found. Do you have any idea how valuable a complete T. rex skeleton would be?"

None of us responded.

"Beyond purchase," he answered himself. "Which is why I want to own it."

He stroked his goatee faster, and his voice grew in excitement. "It has been tedious, yet simple. First, I needed this tunnel. And it couldn't be a rathole tunnel. Not when the skull alone is six feet high. I needed a tunnel wide enough for the truck to carry those massive bones. That took months. Then, bone by bone, I've transported the skeleton here from its original site on Fred Chrisman's land."

"But—"

"But why hasn't any of it been reported missing from the site?" he asked, interrupting me.

I nodded. It was what I'd meant to ask.

"Foolish child," he said. "None of it *is* missing. At least according to appearance."

He chuckled with enjoyment. It sounded like he'd never had a chance to brag about this to anyone before.

"First of all, I'm in charge of the dig. If I don't want something reported, it doesn't get reported. Besides, do you think the skeletons you see in museums are the actual bones? Hardly. They are exact replicas, molded from the original bones, so exact that only an expert can tell the difference. It is only natural that I, the chief paleontologist, would protect such a valuable find by making replicas. I've done that quite openly. Only what people think are the original bones in storage—locked storage which I can access—are, of course, a second set of replicas. The originals are—" Mellonbee pointed beyond me—"the originals are now there, waiting to be covered."

"Covered?" I asked.

"Covered," he said firmly. "To be uncovered years later."

"I don't get it," Mike said. "Years? It seems you've gone to a lot of work. And now you're just going to leave them there?"

Mellonbee shook his head, as if he were sorry for Mike's stupidity. "Years. Maybe a decade. I'll arrange for someone to dig a new well in the trailer park and make sure bits of the fossilized bone show up, enough to get someone digging. By then, I will have purchased all this land and moved it into dummy companies. I'm not going to be as dumb as Fred Chrisman, donating something that valuable. Not when the government or a large corporation will be willing to pay millions for the perfect T. rex skeleton they find below. All that money will go into my pocket for a wonderful, wonderful retirement."

We'd been right about Mellonbee and the land connection. But all along we'd been asking ourselves the wrong question about why. The digging beneath the trailer park was not to take something *out*, but to put something *in*.

"And what's ten years to wait when the payoff is worth millions?" Mellonbee continued. "It will give time for the soil to settle on the bones. I'll be in charge of the new dig, of course, so no one will have suspicions if the bones look a little too arranged. And the longer I wait, the less likely people will connect this T. rex to the one I unearthed on Chrisman's land."

"But someday," I said, "people will find out that the originals are missing!"

"Not when there's a fire at the museum." He was looking at me with a big, big smile. "Not when you and this girl here are found dead in the fire and get blamed for starting it."

His smile widened.

"You might recall, Rocky—if indeed that's your name—we needed a big diversion tonight. Tonight's the night we intend to collapse the tunnel walls and cover the T. rex."

I thought of the bulldozer. Grandfather John and I had

planned to put sugar in the gas tank so it wouldn't work. That way—as Rocky—I had the perfect excuse for not wrecking half the trailer park. We'd hoped to then look around and try to find out what they meant to do. I now knew. But there was no way I'd be able to meet Grandfather John as planned.

"Yes, yes, yes," he said, stroking his goatee with love. "We'll move the rest of your friends up the tunnel and leave them there. Far enough away from the T. rex that no one will find their bones in the ground."

He laughed. "Who knows. In thousands of years, someone might actually uncover their fossilized bones and wonder how they got buried with the dinosaurs."

CHAPTER 26

About a half hour later, after I'd been riding in total darkness with the blindfold tied too tight against my head, David Mellonbee pulled the cloth from my eyes. I blinked, trying to figure out what the pickup truck headlights told me about our location. Seconds later a sign loomed out of the darkness: Royal Tyrrell Museum.

We were there, at the place Mellonbee promised Lisa and me that we would be found dead in a fire. She sat beside me, now without her blindfold, too. Joe was at the steering wheel and David Mellonbee at the passenger side. Between them, with our wrists and ankles taped, we were as helpless as sacks of potatoes.

Back there—somewhere—Mike and Ralphy and Joel sat waiting in darkness for the tunnel support beams to be blown up with small charges of dynamite. At midnight, tons and tons of earth would collapse on them.

Nor did escape seem likely for Lisa and me. We couldn't run. We couldn't fight. I knew the only hope we had was to get our wrists and ankles unbound.

I had a dumb idea. Unfortunately, it was the only idea I could think of. I leaned over and whispered into Lisa's ear.

"What's that?" Joe demanded. He was slowing the truck down to turn from the main road to the long paved drive that led to the museum. "What'd you say to her?"

"Nothing," I said.

"Don't give me that," he said. "Tell me what you told her. I don't want any tricks."

So far it was working just the way I hoped.

"I asked her what she wanted for Christmas."

"Likely story. Tell me what you said, or I'll rip your ear off."

I sighed deeply, like he truly was forcing it out of me. "I told her that at least our parents would know we hadn't started the fire."

Joe laughed. "You'll take the blame, all right. They'll find your bodies inside. They'll find the scorched gasoline can. They'll even find the note we made you write explaining why you did it."

I whispered again to Lisa, like I was privately disagreeing with Joe.

We passed the giant dinosaur sculptures at the front of the museum. Their shadows were eerie in the moonlight. A few seconds later we pulled up to the staff parking lot of the museum. Joe turned off the motor. In the silence, David Mellonbee spoke.

"What makes you so certain you won't take the blame?" Mellonbee asked.

"Nothing," I said. "You guys are right. It's the perfect plan."

"Joe," Mellonbee said casually, "don't rip his ear off. Take your pocketknife and do some damage to the girl."

"All right, all right," I said quickly. "It's the tape."

I felt a shudder of horror saying the rest. "I've seen enough television about criminal investigations to know that they'll send in doctors to check our bodies. The plastic will melt into our skin as our bodies burn. The cops will know our wrists and ankles were taped together. It's called forensics. They'll know someone put us in there."

I waited for their reaction, feeling like I was watching a fish nose at a worm on my hook.

"Cord," Joe said. "We'll use cord or string. That should burn instead of melt. Too bad, punk. There's no way out."

That was the nibble. It wasn't much. But it meant for a moment or two we would be untied. It was all I could ask for.

"I'll get their ankles right now," Joe said, digging into his pocket for a small jackknife. "If I've got to untape them, I might as well have them walk instead of carry them."

A few minutes later he pushed us out of the truck.

The parking lot was empty and quiet. A million stars seemed to fill the black sky. There was some chirping of insects. I guess thinking I was about to die made everything seem much more beautiful, and I ached for a chance to enjoy the night sky again.

Joe carried a can of gasoline from the truck. David Mellon-bee kept a firm grip on my collar and Lisa's, and he pushed us ahead. We walked in silence toward the museum. Toward our deaths.

Using a key from a set on a big key ring, David Mellonbee opened a door at the back of the museum. A high-pitched beeping greeted us. He stepped inside quickly and punched in some numbers on a security pad. Instantly the beeping stopped.

"Bring them inside and shut the door," Mellonbee told Joe. "Guard them here. I'll get some cord from my workbench."

"Sure."

Joe pushed us inside and shut the door behind us. Mellonbee used his key to lock it again. He hurried toward a steel door farther down the hallway.

Joe looked at us and grinned. He waved his pocketknife.

"Punk," he said to me, "you should consider yourself lucky we're leaving you in a fire. If I had my way, I would have done some major hurt to you first. But that forensics stuff means I have to let you die in one piece."

I was disappointed that Mellonbee had actually locked the door behind us. It reduced our chances of escape. Big time.

"Sit and don't move," Joe told me. "That way if you try something funny, I can stop you."

I sat. Lisa remained standing. Joe, it seemed, wasn't worried about her. Which was good.

Joe leaned forward and sliced through the tape around my wrists. I wriggled my fingers.

"Enjoy your freedom while you can," he said.

He turned and sliced through the tape around Lisa's wrists.

It was now or never.

I glanced at Lisa and nodded. I sneezed.

That's what I'd really been whispering to Lisa in the truck: *"When I sneeze, scream and run."*

She screamed. It nearly burst my ear drums. At the same time, she kicked Joe in the shins and jumped around him. If Mellonbee had left the door unlocked, she could have escaped that way. Instead, she had to run toward the center of the museum.

Joe grunted and hopped.

I rolled and jumped to my feet, chasing after Lisa.

"You've got no place to go!" Joe shouted. "Give it up."

We didn't give it up.

I ran as fast as I could, dodging in and out of exhibits. Joe thundered behind us.

"I'm going to make you pay!" he shouted.

I had no doubt he would make us pay. I had no doubt there was no place to go. But all I needed was five seconds without him seeing me.

Lisa and I burst into the room with the tyrannosaurus rex on display. We had only a short head start. Would that buy me enough time?

"Hide," I hissed to Lisa.

She ducked behind an exhibit. I skidded to a stop behind her. I crouched, reaching up my right pant leg.

"If he gets close," I panted, "bolt from here. Distract him."

"Okay." I was glad she didn't ask why. I didn't have even a second to spare for explaining.

Carefully, very carefully, I felt the numbers on the dial pad of the cell phone I had strapped to my leg. I didn't want to risk looking, in case Joe got close enough to see what I was doing.

Nine. One. One.

"There you are!" he shouted, running down at us at full speed.

"Run, Lisa!"

She ran. He swerved to catch her.

I took a quick peek at the cell phone and punched *send*. I wasn't even able to check the display to see if I had the right numbers.

Joe scooped Lisa up in his massive arms. He lifted her and held her in the crook of his right arm. She squirmed and kicked but he held her without effort.

"Come over here, kid," he said to me. "Or I break her ribs."

I stood and moved to him.

With his left arm, he swung low and hard, hitting me in the stomach.

"That'll learn you, punk. Now march back to the door."

He set Lisa down and shoved us both roughly. We stumbled our way past the exhibits.

"We could use some help," I said. Loudly. Like I was terrified. Which I was.

"Shut up, kid," Joe snarled.

"I don't want to die here in the museum," I shouted. "Please don't burn us with all the dinosaurs!"

"I said, shut up!"

"What's all the noise?" Mellonbee asked as we reached the hallway. He held short pieces of rope and was walking toward us.

"Under control," Joe said. "They thought they could get away."

"Please," I said. "Please don't kill us here. The museum is too scary!"

Joe cuffed my head. "Silence."

"But—"

He cuffed me again.

"Ow! That hurt! We're just innocent kids!"

"You're dead kids," Joe said. "Shut your mouth or I'll hit the girl."

I shut my mouth.

Joe tied our wrists and ankles together with cold, machine-like efficiency. I was conscious of the cell phone strapped to the back of my calf. All Joe had to do was brush against it and he would know it was there. . . .

He finished tying the bonds.

"Good and tight?" Mellonbee asked.

"How tight does it need to be?" Joe laughed. "They'll be fried like chickens within ten minutes."

He picked us up—one under each arm—and carried us into the storage room. He looped another piece of rope around our wrists and tied us to the workbench.

Around us it was like a miniature warehouse. Rows of shelves of all sizes. Bones. Boxes. A worktable. Dusting brushes. Cans of glue. Open textbooks.

David Mellonbee went over to a window and unlatched it. "It'll look like they came in through here." He turned and looked at us. "They'll find the note outside."

Joe dumped us on the floor in the middle. He poured gasoline in a circle around us. He sloshed more gasoline over the workbench. On the shelves.

"A fire here," he said, "won't go beyond the fireproof walls into the museum and its security system. All we need to do is burn all the replicas of the bones from the Chrisman find. And you."

He grinned and pulled a small candle out of his vest pocket.

He lit it and turned it upside down so that wax dripped on the floor, about twenty feet from us. Then he stuck the candle upright in the soft wax base and held it until it stood by itself.

He poured more gasoline onto the floor around the candle. Finally he took some paper from the workbench and crumpled it into a small, tight ball. He leaned the paper against the burning candle.

Joe and David walked back to the door.

David Mellonbee stopped and smiled.

"We're going to lock the door so it looks like you guys accidentally trapped yourselves. You got lost in the smoke and couldn't find the window," he said. "Just a few minutes from now, the candle will burn down enough to light the paper and gasoline. When that happens, good-bye."

They turned the lights off and shut the door.

Even if the call had gone through to 9-1-1, even if the operator had heard enough of what I had shouted, even if the operator decided it was a real call and not a prank call, even if police and firemen were on their way...

In the darkness, all Lisa and I could do was stare at the flickering flame of the candle. Too far away to blow out. Getting closer and closer to the paper that would ignite the entire room into a fireball.

Then, in the quiet of their departure, Lisa and I both heard a tinny, distant voice.

"Hello?" the little voice said. "Hello? We're still on the line."

I nearly fainted with relief.

"Operator!" I said, trying to lean down toward my leg. "Is that you? We're still here! Have you sent the police? How long till they arrive?"

CHAPTER 27

The Royal Canadian Mounted Police arrived less than a minute later. Because the 9-1-1 operator was in touch with them, she was able to tell them about the unlatched window. If the police had been forced to break in and try to reach us through the hallway instead of quickly getting in the window, it would have been too late.

As it was, the first Mountie in through the window reached the crumbled paper just as the candle flame was about to touch. If they'd been thirty seconds later, the room would have burst into flame, and all the police would have been able to do was watch helplessly from outside.

The second Mountie found the light switch.

They were both big men—clean shaven, broad shouldered, and very polite to us. As they worked at untying us, the first one asked me to explain. Who. How. Why.

"Sir," I said, "I'll tell you everything I can, but right now our friends are in big, big trouble."

He arched a questioning eyebrow.

"Somewhere," I said, "they're in a tunnel. It's supposed to collapse on them at midnight. The guys who did this to us have set it up there, too."

The two policemen exchanged looks.

The second one spoke to his partner. "I wouldn't have believed this unless I saw it. Besides, you know there's that missing persons' report that John Grant called in on those kids."

"Those are the ones! John's my grandfather!"

The first one spoke. "Where's the tunnel?"

"I don't know for sure," I said. "That's the worst of it. We were blindfolded when they took us in and out. But I can make a guess."

I thought of how they had stopped once for a gate when I was in the back of the truck and then stopped again to enter a building. It could only be one place. A place close enough to hide a bulldozer they would have been using to move some of the dirt inside the tunnel.

"A good guess?" the second one asked.

"It's got to be near Louise Myers' trailer park. Toward the buffalo farm that Mellonbee owns. And there's only one building on that property big enough to hide a tunnel entrance. I think it has a heavy steel door."

"Will they be there—the guys who put you here?"

"No," Lisa said. "The explosion is on a timer. They wanted to get as far away as possible."

"That makes it easier," the first Mountie said. "No worries about a shoot-out."

"Any idea how to get inside?" the second one asked. "It doesn't sound like we have much time to mess around."

"Yup." I grinned. "As a matter of fact, I do have a way."

The clock on the dash of the police car read 11:32. Blue and red lights flashed over the hood of the car and across the pavement as we raced away from the museum.

I directed them. Within minutes the bulldozer was square in the beam of the headlights.

It wasn't until the policemen got out of the car and all of us were visible in the light that Grandfather John stepped out from behind the bulldozer.

"Richard?" he called quietly.

"You didn't put the sugar in the gas tank yet, did you?" I asked. If he'd gotten here too early and done it already, we were in trouble.

"No. I was hoping you would get here. Louise said she hadn't seen you since supper. I called the police. I didn't know what else to do except wait here for you ..."

"Lots happened," I said. Understatement. "But for now, we need that bulldozer."

At any other time, on any other occasion, it would have been a blast to chug across the hills with the police cruiser following. No buffalo in the world would have been brave enough to charge us.

This time, on this occasion, all I could do was fret at how slowly the machine moved. Lisa stood on one side of the driver's seat. Grandfather John on the other.

We have to get there in time.

Lisa reached down and squeezed my hand. I squeezed back. Amazing how a person doesn't need words sometimes.

Finally, a dozen eternities later, the outline of the building rose into sight.

I took a deep breath. The way we'd planned it, I would drive the bulldozer into the doors at full speed and spin to the right. The police car would zoom in behind and straight down the tunnel.

What if my guess is wrong?

I didn't want to think about it. Crashing through the wrong building would be bad enough. But if this wasn't the entrance to the tunnel, I had no idea where to search next. And there were less than ten minutes left until midnight.

The last hundred yards seemed to take another dozen eternities.

Then, crazily, the final ten yards were a blur. Just as Miles had shown me earlier in the afternoon, I lowered the bulldozer blade. The steel doors of the building filled my entire vision.

Boom!

The dozer roared into the steel doors, snapping them open as if they were made of paper.

I pulled hard on the lever, spinning the dozer right.

Brakes! I thought frantically. *Where are the brakes?*

The bulldozer veered toward the wall of the building. I was

barely aware of the blur of the police car as it rushed into the building.

Brakes. Where are the brakes?

Too late. We hit the wall, popping plaster and concrete blocks in all directions.

A second later we were outside again, with tiny pieces of debris showering us.

Lisa leaned over and shut off the ignition key.

I looked behind at a bulldozer-sized hole in the side of a building that was now totally useless, and I could think of nothing to say.

Neither could Lisa or Grandfather John.

There was dead silence, except for the creaking of walls and the fading engine noise of the police car.

It took a moment for the significance of that to sink in.

If the car was still moving, it was going down a tunnel. *We've come to the right spot!*

Ten minutes later Mike and Ralphy and Joel walked out to us at the bulldozer.

"Took you long enough," Mike said.

He's always been the king of gratitude.

"Yeah," Ralphy added. He looked at the mess around us. "By the way, where did you learn how to drive?"

Joel? He hugged me and smiled.

"We haven't been that close, have we, Richard?"

My grandfather and I were walking through a field of wheat, toward the edge of the valley.

"Well, sir," I answered him, "this is really my first day on your farm. With all the other stuff that happened the first few days..."

The other stuff had happened so quickly, it was now difficult to believe any of it had really happened. The Mounties had caught David Mellonbee trying to cross the border. He, in turn, had told them where to find Miles and Joe and their brother in their hideout on a farm about a hundred miles from here. Lawyers and investigators were sorting through all of it. My friends and I would eventually be asked to serve as witnesses.

In short, the Mounties believed Mellonbee's plan might have worked.

He was the expert paleontologist. If people thought the original T. rex bones had been destroyed, and if enough time passed before he "discovered" the new T. rex below Louise's trailer court, and if he was the expert brought in to work on the dig, no one would have known.

My question had been about Mellonbee's choice of land. I thought it would have been easier for him to buy some other land in the river valley and plant the T. rex there. It seemed less complicated than trying to plant it below a trailer court.

Miles had answered that question when the Mounties caught him. He was so angry that Mellonbee had turned them in that he had told as much as he could about it. Miles said that Mellonbee wanted a piece of land with as many people living on it as possible. That way it could cost the government a great deal of money if they wanted to get at the T. rex, money that would eventually go to Mellonbee. The more people who would have to be displaced, the more money involved. The trailer court looked perfect, especially if they could buy it cheap after driving the price down through Miles's and Joe's work.

"No," Grandfather John said, breaking into my thoughts. "What I meant was that I haven't been that close to you and your family over the last few years."

What could I say to that? Especially since it was true.

We reached the edge of the valley. It never failed to impress me how the land just dropped away without warning. It was like walking across a giant tabletop covered with fields of wheat, until suddenly, without warning, you almost stepped into a mile-wide chasm with the ribbon of water at the bottom.

We paused there. I looked down the valley. There were the eroded clay hills of the Badlands, the town of Drumheller a few miles downstream. And, as always, the wide, wide sky above.

"Molly and I stood here every summer evening," Grandfather John said. "We'd hold hands and overlook the valley.

Every summer evening. I miss that woman. She's been gone years now, and I still expect her to walk up behind me this very moment and put her arms around my waist and whisper that she loves me."

He pointed down a steep path. "See how there's a little overlook?"

I did see. The path twisted toward a ledge. From the ledge, it was a sheer drop-off for a hundred feet.

"See that granite marker?"

"Yes, sir."

"She's resting there. We both loved this land and the view. I wanted her to have the valley."

"Yes, sir."

"I don't think you understand," he said. "That woman was everything to me. Some folks marry for convenience. Some for duty. Some because they have a crush on each other that wears out soon after the vows. Molly and me? It was joy and peace all mixed together. Through good times and bad, the love was always there. Not many get the gift like that."

"Yes, sir." I didn't know where to look. Tears were streaming down my grandfather's face.

"She died too young," he said. "Sixty years together would not have been enough, and she got taken from me not long after your mother left the farm. Not only that, she died slow and hard to cancer. Do you have any idea what it's like to watch the woman you love die like that?"

Grandfather John took a long, deep breath to move the trembling out of his voice. "It took the wind out of my sails, son. Took the sunshine right out of my life. It seems like I've just been going through the motions ever since. It's made me a near hermit. I've got the farm and memories of her, and that's all I've wanted around me. It's too painful being around other folks, even your mom and dad. All it does is remind me of what's been taken from me."

There was nothing I could think of to say.

Grandfather John turned his head from me.

In the silence the breeze riffled the wheat behind us. A lone hawk soared in the vast sky over the river. At the far horizon a thundercloud was building to awesome height into the far reaches of the sky, deep purple and more majestic than any mountain.

"Anyway," Grandfather John said, "I thought I should try to explain why I haven't been a close part of your family. It's easier being alone."

He turned back to me. Pain was twisted across his weathered face. "Love hurts, son. That's what I've decided. It hurts. Whatever you love will eventually be taken away from you. If events don't take the love, death will. And death is patient. It will always win."

The soaring hawk drifted closer. "Look at that bird," he said. "It doesn't know that death is waiting. Animals are fortunate that way. Humans, we're the ones with that burden. We can look forty years ahead and know that time will destroy our bodies, then finally take our last breath. How can you live with any hope or meaning when death is going to take away everything good?"

He rubbed his face. When he dropped his hands, he continued. "Sorry, Richard. Don't let me sour you."

Echoes of the screeching woman in the housecoat bounced through my mind. I remembered my anger at her bumper-sticker religious attitude that all it took to fix everything in life was to loudly believe in Jesus. And, looking at the shiny tracks of tears on my grandfather's face, I realized what was most important was hope. Not that faith made life easier, but faith gave it meaning.

"Grandfather," I said, "what if death isn't the end? What if Someone beat death by dying on the cross and rising again on the first Easter? If death doesn't win, won't love be waiting for you on the other side?"

"Are you preaching?" he asked with a half smile.

"No, sir. Just asking. Nobody can make you believe. But I guess either God is there or He isn't." I was thinking out loud, trying to find words to something I'd never needed to put into words before. "You've been talking about love. I guess if the universe is just an accident—you know, hunks of material that just happened to form planets with smaller hunks of matter that just happened to become animals and humans through evolution—then I wonder how something invisible like love got put into the whole system."

I shrugged, almost an apology, because I didn't want to seem like I was telling him what to think. "Looking at love, I think it's a lot harder to choose God doesn't exist than to believe in the simple truth that He and His love are behind everything."

Grandfather John squeezed my shoulder. "Maybe I needed to hear that," he said. He stared off over the valley. "How about you leave me alone now."

"Yes, sir," I said.

I began to walk back toward the farmhouse, where Mike

and Ralphy and Joel and Lisa were waiting. I couldn't shake my sad mood.

As I got closer, I heard shouting from inside the house.

Then I saw Joel burst through the back door. He was clutching the camcorder to his chest. He disappeared around the corner of the house. Wherever the little rascal was headed, I knew he wouldn't be found. All he needed was a head start to escape until he wanted to be seen again.

My sad mood started to lift.

Seconds later Mike came flying through the door, screaming for Joel.

I grinned. Mike had a towel around his waist and was dripping water. He flew down the steps and kept running, clutching the towel with one hand.

"Joel!" he screamed. "Give me that camera!"

I grinned wider. If our shot of the flies lifting the Popsicle stick didn't win us any money on *America's Funniest Home Videos*, I had a hunch that Joel's latest video work would give us another good chance at it.

Of course, we'd have to catch him first.